COMANCHE AND THE MEX GIRL

GABY PRATT

Cover Art:
Michelle Crocker

http://mlcdesigns4you.weebly.com/

Publisher's Note:

This is a work of fiction. All names, characters, places, and events are the work of the author's imagination.

Any resemblance to real persons, places, or events is coincidental.

Solstice Publishing - www.solsticepublishing.com

Comanche and The Mex Girl
Gaby Pratt

Dedication:

For Pete, always.

Chapter One

The jangling mule traces, the grinding wheels of the last transport wagon lumbering out of Fort Richardson bound for Fort Griffin pitched laundress Elena Wade into an anxious state of mind. The hindmost wagon to head out and she was not aboard. Drawing a long breath, she forbade herself to tremble. She knew her choice was fraught with danger.

Callused palms and reddened fingers clasped the wooden cross dangling from a rawhide thong about her neck. *Holy Mary, Mother of God, please forgive me for the things I have stolen for my journey. Please—*

"Hey, Mex girl!"

Elena waited on the hospital's broad veranda for the Senior Corporal motioning from the parade ground flagpole to join her. She appeared doll-size in a faded indigo skirt, white peasant blouse with a bright red sash tied at the waist. Coal-black hair from a center part flowed past her shoulders. "Good day," she said in a cautious manner.

"Why ain't you left yet?" the corporal asked, curiosity lacing his voice. "I thought all you washer-gals had parted for Fort Griffin."

Elena fidgeted with the sash. "The paymaster paid me extra to finish the hospital laundry."

"Fort Griffin's a pretty rough place. What's left of the buffalo hide hunters trade there," the soldier warned.

She stared past his shoulder to the abandoned barracks beyond. "I'm not going to Griffin."

"Fort Concho?" he asked, taken by surprise.

Elena shook her head. "When Doctor Farrar learned Fort Richardson was closing he tried contacting my relatives in Santa Angela, but they have scattered. He found my papa. I am going to join him."

The soldier nodded and glanced around at the all but deserted garrison. "Spooky, ain't it?"

Elena rubbed her arms. "I was thinking so myself."

"With all them Injuns on the reservation, I guess our protection ain't needed. Cap'n says moving on to Griffin widens the frontier. Course now, come a full moon some of them Comanches are liable to sneak off the reservation and do some raiding."

Elena shuddered. Too many stories of depredations had circulated Fort Richardson. She didn't want to think of red savages. The corporal touched two fingers to his cap and returned to lower Old Glory for the last time. His parting shot, "I'm still a-lookin' out for 'em," sent shivers up her spine.

By habit Elena smoothed and tucked the sheets. Leaving the basket in full view on the veranda to be picked up by the staff, she scurried round the back of the hospital and followed the path to Sudsville, the name given to the laundresses' living quarters. The tents had been carted away exposing a clear view of Lost Creek. The yellow ground spotted with old campfires and litter left behind conjured up a reminder of the decision she'd made.

Fort Griffin is not safe. The soldiers had said it was a rendezvous for thieves, and outlaws and a watering hole for gamblers. She'd been dodging encounters of the worst kind since she was twelve and now at sixteen she knew she'd be an easy target.

As a survivor in wretched destitution Elena couldn't resist kicking aside the discarded rubbish. Old copies of the *Frontier Echo*, a rusted harmonica and remnants of a tattered blanket were of no use to her. The broken mirror under a cracked kettle brought a smile. Perfect, she thought, wiggling the glass loose. She turned the dagger-shaped shard over in her hand.

Elena scanned the area and found nothing more to salvage. A fearful thrill mounted. She had to hurry. The road to Doctor Farrar's was not the place she wanted to be after dark.

At the edge of the creek and from the base of the tallest cottonwood she counted off four steps to the partially buried sandstone marking the spot. On her hands and knees she dug away with the sharp-edged shard.

Ten inches down into the spongy earth she scraped the cartridge box lid. Prying the container loose, she then removed the two gold coins inside. The very coins she'd found tangled in the hospital sheets.

If she'd turned them in every patient in the hospital would have claimed them like they had tried to claim her. Remembrance of hands reaching out to grope her as she walked through the hospital brought on a grimace. *The Texans call me greaser like I am nada, dirty, no good. Goliad and the Alamo shaped their hearts. Now they despise all Mexicans. Texans do not hang for killing Indians or Mexicans.* The injustice of lumping Mexicans with Comanches boiled the mixed Mexican-Anglo blood running in her veins.

She slipped the coins in her pocket, dropped the box in the hole, and toed sand over the top. From a tunnel created by a blighted mesquite, Elena pulled out a dented canteen. Next, she tugged free a bedroll fashioned from an old quilt and secured at each end with army belts. She wiggled her hand between the folds and brushed the walnut grips of the Army Issue Colt, one bullet in the chamber. The very Colt she'd stolen from the supply room.

Swish... crunch... snap... silence...

Hovering over the bedroll, she sneaked a peek from side-to-side. Nothing moved. The air was still. She couldn't explain it. It was if she was being watched. Someone knew.

Swallowing a lump of thievery guilt, she hiked the canteen strap over her shoulder. Bedroll hugged to her chest, she retreated up the bank. Before passing through Sudsville for the last time, she glanced back at the remaining scraps of life littering the edge of Lost Creek.

***

Nakiguaht, a lone Comanche, lurked on the far side of Lost Creek. The damp brush steamy from the sun's glare caused the buckskin shirt and fringed leggings to cling to his sinewy body. Mosquitoes and black gnats buzzed and bit, but it was the pin pricks of lights dancing on his eyelids that caught his attention. His first thought, bluecoats signaling. Found off the reservation he'd be shot.

Stealthy as a bobcat he inched closer to the bank and peered between the reeds. The sight took his breath. Never in all his seventeen summers had he expected this. So entranced by the beauty digging with a looking glass he near lost his footing.

What treasure had the little charmer dropped in her pocket? Magic? A stone? Beads? If he had the cover of darkness, he would come upon her and find out for himself.

Following her movements from his side of the creek, he watched as she scampered along the bank to a twisted mesquite. The swish of the little blue skirt, the gentle sway of her hips, the way her raven hair tumbled about her face like a waterfall brought on a smile. As she turned to leave he caught the look of a young warrior possessing courage in battle.

Nakiguaht returned to hide and wait to make his move. Melancholy seeped into his bones at the thought of Fox Eye, his father, on the Fort Sill reservation. A once proud warrior stripped of the Comanche way was dying of the disappearing sickness. He would bring back ponies stolen from under the white eyes' noses. *Father will laugh. It will be good medicine for him.*

Amusing himself, he retrieved the pass from the agency tucked under the buckskin shirt, unfolded it and studied the marks. The new agent had gotten his name off the list of friendly Indians, Indians who had given up their warrior ways, and had issued him permission to trade ponies at the Kiowa camp. That is where the agent thinks I have gone.

But where did the beauty go carrying magic in her pocket and a hidden bedroll? Moving like an animal on padded feet, she had slyly disappeared. He knew it was hopeless dreaming of her, but he couldn't help himself.

At last the waters of Lost Creek mirrored the moon. It was time to check his concealed dun pony, untie the catching rope from the saddle, and hook it over his shoulder. A finely honed Mexican knife clamped between his teeth, a feather dangling from the hilt, he soundlessly waded into the creek.

On the grounds not a bluecoat, horse, mule, or camp dog broke the eerie silence. The animal smells in the barren stables not more than a day old were the most puzzling of all.

Backtracking, he mounted, gave Jacksboro a wide berth and headed west in search of a stocked ranch. Keeping his heels to the pony's flanks, he crossed the vast, flat terrain.

Across the way a dog barked. Clouds drifted past the moon revealing the outline of a ranch. Searching for prey, a night hawk circled above. Nakiguaht took the predator as a sign and hid the dun beside the creek bordering the ranch.

Chapter Two

Keeping to the side of the road, Elena trudged the half mile to Jacksboro. The wide road through town took her past picket shanties, saloons, a sandstone courthouse, and a jailhouse in the final stages of construction. Dodging in and out of the dwindling afternoon traffic of horses, mules and carts, she hurried along.

At the far side of town she veered west. The gritty, deep-rutted road cut through a cattle company layout. A freight wagon loaded with supplies pulled by mules, four up, passed. The driver paid her no mind. Before the dust had settled, she made the sign of the cross and released pent-up breath. *Doctor Farrar's ranch is near*, she thought, and for that she was grateful. Full dark was coming on.

The closer she came to her destination, the more her mind centered on her friend, Doctor Farrar, the best civilian doctor at the fort. *It is said his wife is saintly. I trust him not to cheat me on a horse sale. He will try to talk me out of meeting my father at the cattle crossing. He will warn me it is too dangerous. I will tell him it is my chance to see the American father I have never known.* Matters needed to be settled.

The doctor's name burned on a weathered arrow-shaped board pointed to the narrow road breaking off from the main way. She could see the zigzag fence and the corner of the home of native stone.

Her heart thumped against her ribcage. Maybe she'd made the wrong decision. *I would not be here if Auntie Rosa and Uncle Manuel had not moved closer to Fort Concho for protection. Then cousin Alita would not have married the Buffalo soldier. When he was transferred to Richardson, Auntie Rosa said I had to go with Alita because I was strong.*

Elena swiped at a tear. *Alita did not survive. Not*

even with me there to help. Now Alita is in the cold, cold ground and there is no one to visit her grave.

The kind padre who had started her on *ingles* letters and numbers had enabled her to pick out words from the letter Doctor Farrar had received from his friend. The letter that had revealed Manuel and Rosa Ortiz had departed to the New Mexico territory, exact location unknown. Her father, Neely Wade, had hired on with a cattle drive headed for Newton, Kansas, due to cross the Red River early June.

Elena picked up her step. At last she rounded the bend in the narrow road and faced the full view of the stone house hugged by a wrap-around veranda. Not a lantern shined in the window. No smoke curled from the chimney.

"*Hola* to the house," she called to the imposing structure.

The silence accentuated the corralled horses nickering. She could hear them pawing. A shaggy yellow cur appeared out of the looming shadows. Hackles raised, he nosed the tops of her worn shoes.

"Easy, *amigo*," she coached, letting him sniff her hand. The dog's amicable reaction removed any threat. Relieved, she petted the top of its head.

Above the darkened house sooty clouds scudded past a three-quarter moon. Like silver fingers the rays outlined the house, the zigzag fence, sheds, a well, stables, and corral. Murky shadows took on shapes of oversized ferocious animals. Her whole body tightened while her brain fired doubts fast and furious.

Where is Doctor Farrar? Mrs. Farrar? Are they visiting and I missed them? Is he with a sick patient? Panic rising, she checked over her shoulder at the two dark shapes in the corral. Someone will come to take care of them. It is known he takes great pride in his horses. I will wait.

"Come, *perro*," she murmured and headed for the protection of the stables. Close to her heels, the mongrel followed. Once inside she hunkered down against the wall opposite an empty stall. A yearling and a sorrel horse were bedded down at the end. An old mule collar and a bridle hung above her head, the reins tickling her ear. She scooted over.

From the bedroll, she removed the Army Issue Colt and tucked the weapon in the red sash. Nose pressed to the patched quilt, the dog sniffed. Fingering inside the quilt, she pulled out a loaf of partially molded army bread. Drooling, the dog accepted a broken-off morsel.

Elena wanted to relax, but it wasn't to be, not when she couldn't keep her mind still. The dangers Sergeant Powers pointed out kept sneaking in. *He'd said if my papa's herd was headed for Newton, Kansas, they would cross the Red River at Red Station. Go east to Decatur,* he'd told her, *and pick up the Chisholm Trail.* Elena shut her mind to his warnings of outlaws, Indians and the perils of a girl traveling alone.

The dog growled. The stabled horse and the yearling whinnied. Aided by his nose the cur wiggled open a crack in the wide stable door and disappeared.

Her heart beat wildly. Death grip on the gun handle, Elena peered around the door jamb. Silhouetted against the gray of first light, the black gelding wavered on his hind legs. His front hooves slashed at the sky. Behind the gelding, a sorrel mare, belly swollen with foal, trembled.

Elena knew it was up to her to get the loco gelding out of the corral before he harmed the distressed mare. Doctor Farrar would want her to protect his stock.

She raced back and grabbed the bridle. Hands shaky, she tested the reins to satisfy herself of their strength. Now was not the time for stressed leather to snap.

***

Nakiguaht slithered toward the corral fence. The closer he came, the more he liked the looks of a tall, dark horse. The mare in the corral with the gelding would soon foal and slow him down. No lights shined in the windows of the rock house beyond the fence. Even the dog seemed to have disappeared.

Nakiguaht grinned, the thrill of a steal heightening his senses. He almost laughed. *This is too easy. One horse, the tall one, will not be troubling to handle, simple to hide. The rancher would never catch them.* Before his next move, he thanked the night hawk for pointing the way.

Nakiguaht ducked under the bottom railing. The black horse snorted, stomped, and tossed its mane. Fearful the gelding would arouse the household, Nakiguaht let the animal see him.

Softly, he whispered, "Ho, ho, ho." He took a step forward. "Shuh, shuh, shuh."

The horse squealed. Front hooves lifted into the air.

Trapped between the fence and the horse Nakiguaht braced himself. Quick as a lightning bolt from above, a hoof struck him on the shoulder. A knee pounded his right temple. Knocked senseless, he crumpled to the ground. He could feel the horse's hot breath on his face and see the whites of his eyes. Propped up on his elbows, he snarled low in his throat at the animal.

The horse pivoted, kicking dirt across his chest. Nakiguaht collapsed. Prone on the ground, he prayed to the Great Spirit for his vision to clear and his strength to return.

Someone was afoot.

Gathering his wits, he feigned death.

Adrenaline surging, Elena ran to the corral. At the gate she stopped cold. The sight numbed her. Breath came in spurts. Her knees stated to give. *Holy Mother of God! A dead savage.* She could not move.

Her day of reckoning had come. Terror whipped through her. Slowly, she turned around. The serenity of the solid stone house showed no signs of feathers, lances, or shields. *If they are here they would have seen me.*

The gun weighed heavy in her hand. Sweat trickled

between her fingers. *One bullet. Could she do it? Could she really take her life?* Her lips clamped tight. *Not unless she had to.*

Cautiously she scrutinized the sheds, the well, and the corners of the stable. She squinted at the trees by the creek beyond the corral. It was quiet, too quiet. She knew the savages would return. They always came back for their dead.

Tail flagged, nostrils flared, the gelding tore around the corral barely missing the sorrel. Legs spread awkwardly, the mare nipped at her side. The black horse slid to a stop, snorted and reared.

Her mind raced; she'd have to work fast. *His friends might return. I will catch this gelding, the mare will settle, and then I will ride out for help. I have seen this horse before. He is Doctor Farrar's favored mount, the one that doesn't like the smell of Indians.*

Bridle slung over her shoulder and the gun in hand, she ducked under the railing and came upon the Comanche, maybe a Kiowa. She didn't know. Heart pounding, she stared into his face. She'd seen dead men carried to the stone morgue behind the hospital, but never a corpse this close. Not a savage with bronze features of strength and a secret expression on his lifeless full lips.

Freeing a thumb from the bridle grip, she made the sign of the cross upon her breast. The hesitation was enough. Nakiguaht grabbed her ankle with one hand, her wrist with the other, squeezing until the gun dropped.

In horror she watched his cocky grin spread, saw him glance at the house. Effortlessly, he rose to full height. He could see her now, all of her. His brows raised; a smile twitched his lips.

Elena refused to flinch. His imposing chest, broad and muscular, strained against the buckskin shirt. Fur-wrapped braids hung like daggers on each side of his powerful shoulders. Fringed leggings molded round thick calves. Cold sweat trickled down her armpits. Her heart thumped against her ribs.

Even the gelding appeared momentarily stunned. The mare thudded to the ground like a Mexican load of brick dropped from the sky.

Her captor made a harsh sound. Terrified, she stumbled backwards tripping on the dangling reins from the bridle.

"Let me go," she demanded, struggling against his restraint.

His utterances, unpleasant and strange, baffled her. Desperate for her life, she fired back, "*No comprende!*"

"Take black to stable," he ordered in her language, holding the gun on her. "Be fast. Mare needs help."

Brain racing with escape ploys, she attempted to wrap the reins around the horse's neck. Swishing the laundry paddle in a steaming load of heavy sheets had given her muscles, but it was of no use. Her short stature, the horse tossing its head, the unruly stutter-stepping, made it impossible.

Nakiguaht left the downed mare to help with the gate. The closer he came, the wilder the horse reacted. Elena had no choice but to back off.

Holding the gun on her, Nakiguaht indicated she was to follow while his free hand gripped the horse's nostrils. Twisting the rubbery flesh, he backed the gelding all the way to the stable and inside the empty stall.

She didn't try to run. Not yet.

Nakiguaht stuffed the weapon in the belt harboring the sheathed knife. Her fear of him was not something he wanted and with a warm smile he lessened the hold on her.

It was enough. Elena broke free. She took off in a sprint for her life, the Comanche one breath behind her. The cold barrel tip touched the back of her neck.

"Mare is in heap trouble." His voice grated against her ear. "We help."

He dragged her through the gate and to the downed sorrel. Covered in sweat, the mare showed the whites of her eyes.

"Move tail," he instructed, rolling up his sleeves. "We work fast."

Elena pulled back a hand full of coarse hair. A tiny hoof emerged. The birth of a new life mixed with fear for her own put her in a suspended state. She had to remind herself to breathe. When the coppery hands disappeared inside the mare a strangled gasp escaped.

"What is wrong!" she blurted.

"The head is turned. I will pull it over the knees." He strained with each word.

The horse heaved, tried to roll. In an attempt to nip her side, the mare raised her head, tensed and collapsed.

"Scratch her hip."

She felt a strong contraction. "Is it soon?"

He scooted away from the mare. Standing, he swung his arms by his side and flexed his cramped fingers. "Yes, soon," he said in a non-threatening voice.

The lack of menace in his tone caught her off guard. Before she could respond the mare heaved. A swooshing sound followed. Elena jumped up and stared at the bundle at her feet.

Moving fast, Nakiguaht tore away the tangled blue membrane birthing sack from the motionless little body. He bit the umbilical cord with his teeth. Elena's eyes bulged. She covered her mouth. Pounding hooves on the lane vaguely registered in the back of her mind.

Nakiguaht raked straggly mucus from its nose and put his right ear to its chest. "It does not breathe," he lamented more to himself than to Elena. He began blowing into the foal's nostrils. Vigorously, he rubbed its ribs. So focused on his actions, she failed to notice the dog taking off down the lane.

Nothing had worked. Aware of incoming riders, he

groaned in frustration. He had one more maneuver to try. He lifted the gangly foal, shook the little body, and then dropped it. The jolt jarred life-giving respiration into operation. Elena blinked in astonishment.

Thumping his fist to his chest, he proudly stated, "I am Nakiguaht."

Instinct told her he wanted praise. But what would he do next? Before she could take action the riders closed in. She watched Nakiguaht hunch in a flight position and glance in the direction of the creek. It was too late. They both knew he was caught.

"Hold it right there," bellowed Doctor Farrar from the horse, his rifle pointed at them. "Elena, what are you doing here?"

Not interested in her answer, the squinty-eyed rancher riding with the doctor curled his lips. "A greaser and a red devil on yer property. Reckon there's any more around?" He stood in the stirrups and scanned the area.

Rifle aimed at Nakiguaht, Doctor Farrar dismounted. After the Rebellion he'd migrated to Jacksboro and married a fine pioneer woman, Martha Huckabee, and now the God-fearing doctor not only practiced at the fort's hospital, but traveled to outlying farms and ranches. Oft times he had only the stars to lead him and a cow trail to follow. It had kept him lean and iron-muscled.

As he approached the Comanche the tail end of his eye caught the new-born foal peeping under the mare's belly. The scrawny rancher, Dan Belcher, continued to cover the doctor's backside ready to fire at anything that moved.

Elena turned to Nakiguaht. "Do not be afraid. Doctor Farrar is a fair man."

The glimpse of his face set her back. This was not the same Comanche of five minutes ago. His eyes stared sullenly as if he'd not understood one word of Spanish she'd spoken.

"What is going on?" Doctor Farrar asked, directing his questions at Elena. "Why are you here? Where did he come from?"

Elena took a deep breath. "I came here on business. The Comanche was in the corral. The mare had trouble. He saved the foal, Doctor Farrar."

Dan Belcher sauntered up in front of Nakiguaht and yanked the Colt poking out from his belt. "Lookee here," he said, waving the weapon in his face. "I'd say it's a brand new Army Issue Colt. Wonder where he stole that?"

Elena drew breath in. Guilt tied her tongue. She couldn't speak.

Doctor Farrar shrugged. "Keep an eye on him while I check the foal."

Elena followed. Out of earshot of the rancher he asked if the Comanche had harmed her.

"It is fair to say he scared me to death, but he did not harm me. His attention was on the mare. He did not forsake her."

Farrar scratched his chin. "Wonder how he got here?"

Elena said, "I did not see a horse."

"Where is Ornery?"

"Ornery?" She did not understand.

"The black gelding."

"We put him in the first stall. He was acting loco."

"He'll let you know if an Indian is around." Frowning at the vultures drawn by the blood gases, he added, "He's saved my bacon a time or two."

The circling scavengers prompted Elena to offer to bury the afterbirth. Farrar thanked her. The shovel, he said, was in the stables.

"You can bury this heathen while you're at it," the rancher snickered. "Any hostile Injun off the reservation is fair game."

"That won't be necessary," Doctor Farrar stated in a

firm voice. "We'll take him into town and hand him over to the sheriff." To Elena he said, "Wait in the house for Mrs. Farrar. She is with Mrs. Speer. She should be returning shortly."

Dan Belcher wanted to know what was wrong with the Widow Speer. Courteously, Doctor Farrar explained she'd been bitten by a spider and had developed a high fever. Mrs. Farrar had stayed to take care of her.

Elena went about the business at hand. Every now and again she sidled a peek at Farrar saddling the stabled horse for Nakiguaht. Dan tied his hands in front of him. There was no need to help him mount. His graceful leap was something to behold.

She needed one more look. Shovel propped against the fence, she hurried toward the slouched figure mounted on Farrar's horse. To her puzzlement he refused to glance her way.

Gathering reins, Doctor Farrar repeated, his voice weary, "Tell Mrs. Farrar to stay inside."

Elena nodded. Her last attempt to make eye contact was lost. Sulking, head downcast, he stared at the mount's withers.

Dan Belcher sneered. "If Widow Speer finds out there's red vermin in town, spider bite or not, she'll hang 'im with her bare hands."

Elena backed away from the mounted trio. She'd never witnessed a hanging, but she'd seen pictures in newspapers at Fort Richardson. It didn't take much to conjure up the sight of a protruded swollen tongue, head cocked to the side, a loose body dangling from a noose. Rattled to the core, she had to fight off the dire image before finishing the task at hand.

On her way back to the stables she couldn't help but puzzle over the Comanche's behavior, the complete change in him. Maybe he was afraid. She shook her head. No, he was more like a trapped wild animal. Her thoughts were turning to the Colt and her cat's tongue when a gust of wind lifted a folded paper by the fence. Midair she snatched on to it.

The first words she read, Indian Agency, were similar to the Spanish words, *Indio Agente*. The cursive signatures were beyond her capabilities. Brows furrowed, she deciphered permission, *permiso*. The filled-in blank looked like hen scratching. It must be the name Naki... Kiowa camp, *campo,* made no sense.

Once again, she studied the printed line at the top. A strange word preceded *Indio lista.* She'd seen the word before, but where? She glanced up at the disappearing vultures. When she studied the word again it jumped out at her. The letter! Doctor Farrar's contact had signed it Your Friend. *Friend,* she repeated. *Friend, friend, Friendly Indian List!*

Not only was he off the reservation, but he had a new army issue Colt in his possession. The very gun she'd stolen. Dan Belcher, alone, would see to it he got a neck-tie partly because of it. If they hung him, his dark, penetrating eyes would haunt her forever. Eyes full of mystery and danger and a smile that had crossed a barrier where life was concerned. This paper from the agency could help. She didn't want to think of what could happen to her. Stolen property had consequences. She'd never expected blood on her hands.

Elena anxiously watched the road for Martha Farrar's arrival. Her reward came just when the agony of waiting had become unbearable. Skirt hiked up, she ran to meet the buggy.

Chapter Three

The depth of kindness in Martha Farrar's china blue eyes put Elena at ease as she explained what had happened.

"Doctor Farrar wishes you to be in the house until he returns," Elena said for the second time.

"And what were you doing here?"

"I came to buy a horse."

Mrs. Farrar's brows shot up.

Touchy Mexican pride came into play. "I have *dinero.*"

Martha Farrar smiled. "I see, but now you think you should go to the jail and turn over the pass from the Indian Agency Headquarters at Fort Sill."

Elena handed the form to Mrs. Farrar. "The Comanche is a friendly Indian. It is printed on the pass."

"The pass gives."—She paused to study the name— "Nakiguaht permission to trade ponies at the Kiowa Camp, not to venture into Texas. That makes him hostile. Lucky he wasn't shot."

"*Sí,* but he is a friendly Indian," Elena repeated, her voice urgent.

She watched Mrs. Farrar dawdle with a stray wisp of dusty brown hair. Captured off the reservation was bad enough, but if the law accused him of murdering for the Army Issue Colt, the very Colt she'd stolen, he'd hang for sure.

"Perhaps the pass will help. As you said he did not attempt to escape. He did save the foal. Take my buggy into town and if William is still at the jail please try to convince him to ride back with you. He's been up all night."

"*Sí, sí,* I will," Elena promised, backing off. "*Gracias*, Mrs. Farrar, *muchas gracias.*" She turned on her heel and ran the rest of the way to the rig.

Perched on the edge of the padded seat Elena gathered up the lines and released the brake. The snappy chestnut mare with flaxen tail and mane responded with a cluck and a single flick of the well-oiled leathers.

On the road leading to Jacksboro the mid-morning hot breeze whipped sandy grit across her face. Unfazed by the peppering, she expertly urged the mare on.

Heads turned as they clip-clopped through town. Elena ignored the gathered crowd in front of the two-storied cut-stone jail under construction. The sight of her emerging from Mrs. Farrar's buggy prompted a barrage of comments. Marching toward the door, she let the stinging insults... greaser... reckon she stole it... roll off her back.

Inside the jailer's room Nakiguaht was slumped against the two-foot-thick walls. Hands untied, he kept them crossed over his knees. By his side Dan Belcher held a squinty eye on him. William Farrar, hip hooked on the corner of the oak desk, looked up in surprise. Big as a draft horse, Deputy Bryson Cox rose from behind the desk.

Light shafts from the barred window glinted off the Army Issue Colt barrel dead center of the scarred furniture. A feather trailed from the knife hilt beside it.

Elena fished in her skirt pocket, removed the pass, and handed it to Doctor Farrar. "I found this after you left," she said. "I think it is important."

William Farrar informed the deputy this was the Mexican girl who'd found the Comanche on his ranch and together they had assisted in a difficult foaling. Hunching his massive body forward, Bryson Cox read over Farrar's shoulder.

"Wish we knowed how he got this Colt. I got me some terrible visions."

Tapping the pass on the desk, William Farrar appeared not to have heard Cox's remark. Instead, he went over to Nakiguaht. Thus far the Indian had not uttered a sound. He asked again how he came to be on his ranch in

English, and then, on a lark, tried to communicate in his limited Spanish. Many had picked up the language from their Mexican captives.

Nakiguaht refused to lift his head. Farrar cupped his chin, raised it for him, and stared into a pair of surly eyes. Defiantly, he jerked free of Farrar's grip, turned sideways and held up the left braid. Lifting his palms and shrugging, he signed deafness.

Elena's lips parted in surprise.

The sight crawled Farrar's flesh. In all his years of practice in the medical profession never had he seen such a scar. His first thoughts were of infection and screw worms followed by admiration for whomever had tended the wound.

"Why not escort him back to Fort Sill and let the Agency deal with it," Farrar suggested. "Perhaps someone there can sort out the situation. No need to provoke his relatives to take revenge. We've had enough raiding. It's time to turn the tide."

"Can't do that, Doc," Bryson Cox said in a gruff voice. "There's this matter of the Army Issue Colt, brand new and fresh out the box."

Elena took a deep breath. She inched her way in front of the desk. "I can solve that," she said in a tone she didn't recognize. "He took it from me."

Propped against the wall next to Nakiguaht, Dan Belcher leaned forward and arched a spit of tobacco into the brass spittoon beside the desk. The ping punctuated the silence.

Bryson Cox demanded to know where this greaser had gotten the Army Issue. Doctor Farrar cleared his throat and, in a manner not to be argued with, stated he'd given it to her for protection.

"Well, then," Cox said, backing down. "I guess mebbe you've got the right idea. The sheriff's in Fort Worth with the mayor getting a contract extension for this here jail construction. People's minds will be eased at the completion. Seeing as he left me in charge I'll get an escort to –"

Outside the jail commotion mounted and spilled over. Widow Speer, face flushed with fever, burst through the door.

"Where's that devil savage?" she shrieked. "He killed my husband. He killed my boy. Hang him! Hang him!"

In two steps Doctor Farrar was by her side. The stout woman endowed with strength honed from frontier living stood rigid as a rock. The veins protruded on her neck. Sprigs of silvery hair splayed wildly about her face framing the pure hatred in her muddy gray, red-rimmed eyes. Farrar attempted to turn her from the Comanche. She would not budge.

"Come on, now, Mrs. Speer," the doctor said, his voice calm and soothing. "You should be in bed."

Nakiguaht raised his head to look at her.

Widow Speer let forth a blood-curdling scream.

Elena flinched and turned aside.

Dan Belcher joined Doctor Farrar. Together they guided the sobbing and shaking Widow Speer. Deputy Cox rounded the desk. Holding the door, he barked at the crowd to back off.

Elena slipped in beside Nakiguaht. She, too, stared at the floor. Despite the high emotions whirling round her, she felt a burden lifted and a blessing received to have Doctor Farrar stand up for her. The business with the Colt being resolved had saved the Comanche from a hanging and cleared her of theft. Deep in thought, she absentmindedly fingered the cross about her neck.

In a move daring detection Nakiguaht snugged his arm against hers. The subtle contact created warmth which caught her off guard. Nakiguaht made a soft deep-throated sound. Keeping his head down, he rasped from the side of his mouth, "My friend, I will not forget."

Face flushed, Elena looked at him in wonder. She started to reply, but checked herself. Giving away his ruse of deafness would only muddy the waters. With the Comanche back on the reservation the matter would be settled peacefully. No twisting at the end of a rope. No eyes haunting her.

Outside the 'hang 'im' taunts subsided to be replaced by disgruntled grumbling. She could hear Doctor Farrar's voice, but not his words. Widow Speer's sobbing quieted.

Doctor Farrar hustled past Cox. Before the door could be shut Dan Belcher squeezed through and took up his place beside the Comanche. Farrar grasped the gun from the desk.

"Come on," he said, handing the weapon to Elena. "Mrs. Speer is with a neighbor. She'll take care of her."

Deputy Sheriff Cox spoke up. "I'll see to it this here Comanche gets escorted to Fort Sill. Ain't nothing but nags at the livery. The extension contract committee took the best of the lot to Fort Worth. I reckon none of 'em left would make it to Sill. You mind him ridin' your horse?"

Doctor Farrar agreed and hurried Elena outside. He made quick work of tying his mount behind the buggy. As she climbed aboard the weight of the gun in her pocket tugged the waistband of her skirt. She sat quietly with her hands folded in her lap as the angry onlookers clustered around the buggy.

"Should've hung the red devil," a voice boomed.

"Yeah. Lookee how upset the Widow Speer got. Ain't no sense in that. Not after what she went through. Now big hoss Cox is goin' to send 'im back to the reservation."

Toby, the local blacksmith, reeking of tobacco and horse sweat, came forward. "I jes want to ask the doctor here how come he thought that heathen was worth saving?"

25

"Come on, Toby," Doctor Farrar cajoled, knowing of his short temper. "The fella's deaf. Let Fort Sill deal with it."

Junior Foy, alcohol on his breath, scowled. "I'd hung 'im on general principles if'n it was up to me."

"Let it be. No need to hang him and stir up his relatives. We've had enough raiding."

Soon the mutterings... Indian lover... bleeding hearts... taken up with a greaser... could be heard. William Farrar glanced at Elena. Neither spoke a word until they were outside of town.

"Doctor Farrar," Elena confessed, "Nakiguaht is not deaf."

"I know." He chuckled.

She smiled. "You lied for me about the gun."

"I'm glad you have it. If I had seen it first I would've taken it and given it to you. Fort Griffin is rough."

"*Sí,* but I'm not going to Griffin. That is why I came to see you. I want to buy a horse."

Doctor Farrar appeared to concentrate on the rhythmic swish of the chestnut's flaxen tail. Elena bided her time. When they pulled up in front of the house, the hired hand, a neighbor boy of not more than eleven, and Martha were at the corral fence admiring the new foal.

At the sight of the buggy coming in, the towheaded youngster ran to the doctor for instructions concerning the animals and chores. Elena went straight to the stables for her blanket roll.

Doctor Farrar joined his wife at the fence. All her earthly possessions clutched to her breast, Elena stood a respectable distance behind them and waited. At her side the yellow cur wagged his tail.

Genuinely curious, the doctor turned and asked, "What is this about buying a horse?"

"I have *dinero.*"

"My horses are not for—"

Martha placed her hand on her husband's arm. "Why do you need a horse, dear?"

"Doctor Farrar wrote to his friend at Fort Concho for information about my family. He could not find my people in Santa Angela, but he learned my papa has hired on with a cattle drive headed for Newton, Kansas. I am going to meet him at Red Station."

Forehead wrinkled, Martha looked to her husband.

"Elena, you can't do that. The trail is far too dangerous for a lone woman. There could be more renegade Comanches out there. Not to mention outlaws, the weather, wild animals."

Elena tucked her head, thought a minute, and raised her face to meet the doctor's. Her eyes burned with determination.

"The trail is not as dangerous as Fort Griffin. I want to be with my papa."

"When was the last time you saw him?"

"I have never seen him. Mama died in childbirth. He gave me to her sister, my Auntie Rosa. Once when I was little she said he'd joined the Rebellion."

"Elena, you are taking a risk. Lives have a way of changing. Even if you find him chances are he won't be able to take you on the drive with him."

"My papa will tell me where I can wait for him."

Exasperated, Doctor Farrar frowned. "But you don't know where on the Red he'll cross."

"Sergeant Powers said if the herd is going to Newton they will cross at Red Station."

Martha slipped her arm around her husband's waist. "You can stay here with us. You will be safe."

"*Muchas gracias,* Mrs. Farrar, but I will find my papa. That is where I belong."

Elena placed the blanket roll at her feet. Her hand slipped into her skirt pocket. Slowly she brought forth the gold coins and held them outstretched in the palm of her hand. "I need to buy a horse."

Catching the skepticism in his eyes, she suffered a pang of guilt. "I found them in the laundry sheets. I did not know who they belonged to so... so I kept them."

Holding her breath, she waited for his judgment. According to Texans all Mexicans were thieves. Trembling, she watched his expression mellow and become pleasantly reflective.

"A good price for Ornery," he teased.

Elena relaxed.

Doctor Farrar placed his hands on his back and stretched. A low groan escaped his lips.

Martha started for the house. "Supper will be ready shortly. Come along, Elena. You must be hungry, too."

The kitchen proved to be both cozy and functional. The silver sugar bowl and creamer on the oak table gleamed. Leather-bound medical books dotted the polished surface. The stocked shelves made her mouth water. When Martha began taking dishes from the china cabinet Elena offered to help.

The aroma of bread and warmed-over stew brought William Farrar to the table. The conversation centered on William reminiscing about his favorite horse. Elena couldn't help but notice the love in his voice.

"One time I was on way back to Jacksboro. It was late. The full moon made the hairs stand up on the back of my neck. Old Ornery raised such a fuss I gave him his head. Damned if the horse didn't take me off the road and into the woods. Not long afterwards a war party of four Kiowas passed by."

"I have heard the solders at Fort Richardson speak of such horses," Elena said.

William smiled. "Ornery is like that. That horse pure hates the smell of Indians. He'll warn you every time."

Over a second cup of coffee the conversation turned

to the Comanche. Farrar had Elena relate the foaling step-by-step.

"But what frightened me," Elena said, "I know he was trying to steal the black. I saw the print of a hoof on his shoulder. I think Ornery knocked him down."

Visibly shaken, Martha spoke softly. "I wonder how he traveled from the reservation to Jacksboro?"

"Who knows? The stamina of a Comanche beats anything I've ever seen. They're clever, too." William chuckled, wagging his head. "Pretending to be deaf took me by surprise."

After William excused himself and trudged off to the bedroom, Elena and Martha tidied up the kitchen. Elena offered to sleep in the stables, but Martha told her that was nonsense and showed her to the guestroom. After lighting the kerosene lamp, Martha quietly shut the door behind her.

Beside the four-poster bed Elena slipped out of her skirt, smoothed the lace-edged pantalets Auntie Rosa had sewn for Alita and unlaced her high-tops wondering how much longer they would last. She pulled back the covers, turned down the wick until the flame disappeared and climbed between the clean sheets. But sleep eluded her. Her brain was far too active from the day's events and the journey she would start tomorrow.

She scooted downward under the covers, hiding her fears in the dark, but the murmurs persisted in the recesses of her mind like they had so many nights before. The whispers hushed behind the curtain about her papa. She had to find him and let him know she – an obtrusive flashback of Widow Speer's wretched wail sneaked in giving her the shivers.

Turning on her side, she tucked the quilt end under her chin. *My friend, I will not forget, is of no matter,* she told herself, tamping down remembrances, his wild smell, and the disconcerting rub of the buckskin. *He is Comanche and I fear him. It is known of their skill with horses. It is hearts they do not have.*

Chapter Four

*D*eputy Sheriff Bryson Cox spent a long night locked inside the jail drinking coffee and worrying about the savage chained to a partially constructed cell. He didn't have a choice. It'd taken the rest of the afternoon to get the Comanche's paper work in order, find escorts to go with him and come up with trail provisions at the Mercantile. Scratching behind his ear, he figured he'd done right deputizing Dan Belcher and Junior Foy.

And now before the citizens of Jacksboro rancher Dan mounted on a paint gelding led the hand-tied Nakiguaht on Farrar's horse out of town. Tagging behind, Junior rode a brown nag displaying a nasty welt on its rump. Enjoying the parade, Junior nodded to the gawkers lined up on each side of the wide road.

Accommodating the haughty stares Nakiguaht worked on a sneer. It was hard to keep from laughing. The white eye called Junior had fire water on his breath and failed to notice the gap between his wrists. Clip-clopping ahead the paint's choppy gait would disgust Fox Eye. The brown was an insult to the palm of the Comanche, best horse stealers.

Side-glancing the settlers, storekeepers and drifters, he did not see the girl called Elena. The one with the silky black hair and eyes the color of new grass who did not give him away. He'd had to touch her. Tell her he would not forget, and now the abiding tenderness of her arm against his would forever be with him.

Farrar's horse had an easy gait, one that required little attention from its passenger, one that gave him time to ponder. *The People do not live well on the Fort Sill Reservation. We are cheated of beef. Women and children wail. Promises of the White Father are broken.* Never would he scar the earth like farmers, never would he police the bands. No longer a warrior, he did not know how he

31

could gain honor to make Elena praise him.

Not much on the trail, Junior Foy had gone without a drink for about as long as he wanted to. The sun had boiled down on them since they'd left Jacksboro and now at full dusk he thought it was time to scout for a camp site. Dan Belcher agreed.

Nakiguaht offered no resistance when the slit-eyed one indicated he should sit at the base of a live oak. He settled as comfortably as he could while bound to the tree.

Later by the campfire the voice of Junior gradually became more and more whiskey-laden. Soon the grumbling round the fire died down and the snoring of a drunk and the stillness of a tired rancher took over.

Freed of the restraints, Nakiguaht rose slowly. Like a wolf instinctively knowing when to move silently and swiftly, or slowly and deliberately, he lifted a rifle, his knife, and a sack of provisions from his sleeping enemies.

Nary a twig snapped or underbrush rustled as he made his way to the creek and cut the paint and brown loose. Mounted on Farrar's sorrel, he headed east. Riding hard all through the night, he hoped to reach the Chisholm Trail before daybreak. Paralleling the Jacksboro-Decatur road, he was getting close.

Comanche patience took over and, knowing he had to rest the sorrel, he camped near a fenced ranch bordering a slim stream. The posts and thin wire would hamper his efforts to take bounty. Here he would wait for darkness and then try for many ponies on the Chisholm.

The sorrel's throat rumble alerted him. Clamping his hand over its mouth, he then backed the horse deeper into the copse but not before he glimpsed the rider on a black pony crossing beyond, a rider with a yellow dog following.

***

Tarrying for the household to stir, Elena spread out

the contents of the old quilt. When the closing of Fort Richardson had become a reality a discard pile destined to be burned began to grow.

Each evening she'd picked through the pile. Handy with needle and thread, she'd repaired a gray flannel army shirt and tailored a pair of tan trousers to fit over her slim hips. Her favorite item was a floppy hat. Her biggest disappointment was not finding a pair of boots.

Nimble fingers quickly plaited a single braid and fastened it to her crown with Alita's silver comb. Tucking stray tendrils under the floppy hat brim, she stared in the mirror above the washstand. On the Chisholm Trail she would pass as a *chico*.

At the thump, thump of Doctor Farrar stomping into his boots and the muted voice of Martha, she gave one last smoothing of the covers and headed for the kitchen.

Martha's eyes popped.

Reared back in a chair William Farrar came forward. "Don't do this, Elena," he said. "Have you considered how dangerous this trip will be? You could lose your life. Perhaps I could find you a job in town."

"Doctor Farrar, I belong with my papa." The finality in her voice left no room for argument.

To ease the growing tension between her husband and Elena, Martha asked, "Dear, what can we do to help?"

Elena broke out in a smile. Pulling the coins from her pocket, she then placed them beside the doctor's plate. "Tell me what I need to know about my new horse, Ornery."

Doctor Farrar knew he was licked. If not his horse then one from the horse trader in town and she'd be no match for him. A reliable mount was the best he could offer while Martha couldn't offer enough. She filled an old saddlebag with sacks of coffee, flour, salt, a small frying pan, and a slab of bacon. She found room for leftover breakfast biscuits, ham, a tin cup, and a box of lucifers.

William Farrar tacked Ornery in a spare saddle and bridle and hooked a canvas sack of grain on the horn. Tugging Ornery's forelock, he clucked as much to himself as to the horse. Love mixed with regret filled his eyes. Nonetheless, he removed a pad and pencil from his pocket, scratched out a bill of sale, and handed it to Elena. Reluctantly, he accepted the coins thrust in his hand.

Elena clutched her breast in dismay. "I cannot pay for supplies too."

"You helped save my foal," he reminded her. "That's more than enough pay."

He hoisted the blanket roll behind the saddle and reached for the leather ties. Martha handed up a woolen blanket, gray with a black border. Over his shoulder he asked, "Sure you won't change your mind?"

Elena gave him a tight smile and shook her head.

"All right, then," he said, resignation in his voice. "Let me tell you about Ornery."

He went over the horse's good habits and bad, his likes and dislikes, especially his favorite dislike, the smell of Indians. If one is around Ornery would let her know. He made a rumbling sound in the back of his throat as an example.

Elena thanked and hugged her benefactors. Doctor Farrar started to offer a leg up, but Elena, unassisted, was already in the saddle. A flurry of good-byes, good lucks, and write to us overlapped each other.

Elena didn't trust her voice. Nodding, she turned the horse toward the lane and from a slow walk advanced to a trot. She was at the bend in the lane before she noticed the yellow cur following her.

Checked up, she reprimanded the dog and started off again. The dog kept to Ornery's heels. After a few steps she stopped and looked back at the house. William Farrar and his wife waved. She pointed to the dog.

Doctor Farrar cupped his hands around his mouth

and shouted, "Take the dog with you."

Elena wasn't sure she'd heard correctly until he motioned a go-ahead with his hand. She started off again. After rounding the bend, she pulled up and looked down at the dog. Tail thumping, he sat beside the horse. When she picked up a trot he took up his place behind the horse.

Martha murmured, slipping her arm around his waist. "There goes your dog."

"I never had one to follow a horse like he does. Something in his blood, I guess." William chuckled. "Then again, the grub in the saddle bag might be an incentive."

"Think they'll make it to Red Station to meet her father?"

Admiration mixed with trepidation in his voice, William sighed. "It'll take a miracle."

Elena felt good. The road to Decatur, east of Jacksboro, had been used to transport supplies to Fort Richardson. It was thought to be safe. Bouncing kids in the back of a buckboard passed and pointed at the dog. She heard the little girl squeal he looked like a lion.

Smiling to herself, she pressed on. A rider on a mule, hat brim flapping to the jogging gait, glanced admiringly at Ornery.

It was the hard case, a rifle under his knee, holstered side arms tied low, galloping towards her that put fear in her heart. Readying to bolt, she inched her hands upwards on the reins.

The ends of his navy bandana about his throat flagged each side of his shoulders. Hat brim tipped back revealed a pair of lecherous eyes raking her as he passed. She twisted in the saddle making sure he was keeping on.

Catching her looking back, he yelled, "Nancy-boy!"

Jerking back round, she picked up her pace until the chilling laughter and the thundering hoof beats faded away. The encounter sent a signal she had to be on guard at all times.

It was getting late. A stand of trees on the rolling terrain indicated water and good cover. Veering from the road, she broke into an easy lope. The grass met Ornery's hocks in places, knees in others. She checked over her shoulder for the dog.

Beyond the stream a ranch surrounded by miles of plank fence and smooth wire indicated prosperity. She could smell cattle. Here she would camp out of sight. Saddle for a pillow, canteen filled and the Colt within easy reach, Elena wound herself up in Martha's gray blanket.

"Dog," she whispered as if someone would hear. "I do not recall your name."

Tail thumping, he drooled. Stream water dripped off his shaggy mane.

"I will call you León." Close to his ear, she confided, "You do look like a lion."

Oblivious to his new name, León wolfed down his share of ham and biscuits.

Moonlight dappled through the leafy treetops. The night air chilled. She snuggled tight in the woolen covering. Her body tensed. She began to worry. Four dollars was all she'd saved from her wages. Part of it had belonged to Alita. Tomorrow she'd buy cartridges in Decatur.

Twisting and turning, she couldn't settle. The journey ahead played on her imagination. She tried in vain to tamp down the agony of why her papa had never contacted her. Auntie Rosa would not answer her questions. Alita did not know.

León curled up atop her feet and soon snored away. The smell of the wet animal nearly took her breath, yet she did not disturb him. Anchored by the dog her body stilled.

Sleep followed.

Time passed.

Ornery's throat rumbled.

Elena woke with a start. León scrambled from her. Snarling, he took off. Ornery's scream pierced the thick night air. Beyond the wire fence a ranch horse answered.

Clutching the Colt, she eased from the blanket. Footsteps rustled behind her. Blood drained from her face.

A voice rasped, "*Mi amigo.*"

Whirling around in the direction of the voice, Elena held the gun with both hands. Arms extended, she hissed, "You cannot steal my horse."

Leading the sorrel, Nakiguaht stepped from behind cover ignoring the weapon pointed at him. "Tie him next to the black. It will calm him, or we will be discovered."

Caught with a renegade Comanche would be the death of both of them. Frightened, but not so much out of her wits, she gripped the weapon tighter. Accepting the sorrel's reins with her free hand, she backed off towards Ornery.

One handed, she wrapped the reins around a low limb. She turned to make a stand, but Nakiguaht had vanished. Franticly she scanned the area. Stingy moon illuminations blurred black tree trunks. A stump looked like a crouched bear.

"The night breeze will take my scent away from the black over here." His voice was soft and eminently reasonable.

Elena jerked around. So close, face to face, she could see his firm features, the confident set of his broad shoulders. His smile set her off.

"Where are your escorts?" she demanded.

"I left them sleeping."

Her strong voice faltered. "Are they dead?"

"No. I escaped," he said with a cocky grin.

That did it. Anger mixed with chilling fear raced to the surface and erupted like a volcano. "You are a scoundrel!"

"I have been called red devil, heathen, red vermin, savage by the Texans. Scoundrel? That is a new name."

She gave him a critical squint. "Doctor Farrar stood

up for you. He suffered a shunning at the jail on account of it and that was not right. He is a good man."

In defense of her barrage he lifted his left braid, turned up the palms of his hands and shrugged.

"Doctor Farrar knows you are not deaf," she said part in disgust, part in alarm.

He continued to shrug. Shoulders thrust back she nudged his broad chest with the gun nose. "Leave, or I will shoot."

León prodded between them. Off balance her cheek brushed against the right braid otter fur. Refusing to be intimidated by his chortle, she yanked the braid upwards. "There's nothing wrong with this ear!" she screeched.

Stunned, Nakiguaht was momentarily immobilized. Temptation for the beauty of Lost Creek overpowered. A slow smile spread. Taking on the nature of a wolf pack leader, confident and decisive, he made his move. Gathering her small frame, he held her close to his body. His eyes alone betrayed his ardor. His arms were too busy holding on to the cougar and dodging the wavering weapon.

Chapter Five

Neely Wade hadn't thought of the baby in almost twenty years and then that captain from Concho started asking questions in the saloon. Damn sumbitch. He'd heard his name mentioned and left. To calm his nerves, he started in on *Come a ti yi yippy, yippy yay, yippy yay, come a ti yi, yippy, yippy yay.*

"Neely Wade's coming in," Tate Hagan, the cook, said, hoisting the chuck wagon tongue towards the North Star.

The wrangler, a string bean of a youth dubbed Bud, a first timer on the trail, hung a lantern on the tongue. "His voice sure does haunt a body."

Tate bent over the coffee pot to check the hot coals. Capping his rheumatic knees with his large hands, he hesitated before rising.

"I hear'd tell he made a lead steer cry once," he replied as serious as if he was praying in church.

Bud grinned. He'd been at the bottom of every prank, joke, and leg pulling since the drive had started.

"Only one thing," Tate shared confidentially, "I hate going through the Indian Territory with him. He don't take kindly to them Red men. It brings out the fire in 'im."

Bud paused and looked in the direction of the mournful singing. "I'll say this for Neely Wade. He's the best atop a horse I've ever seen."

Tate chuckled. "Seems to me he gits along better with hosses than he does with people."

The incoming pounding hooves halted the conversation. Horse taken care of by the young wrangler, Neely Wade joined Tate.

He was a tall man with long sandy hair and a pair of piercing green eyes that'd caused many a hard case to turn aside. Orphaned at a young age, he was taken in by a Mexican family near the border. The time spent with them had long since faded from memory.

Hunkered by the fire, Neely Wade built a cigarette. Pouring hot, black coffee into a tin cup, he first blew on it before testing a swallow. Dancing shadows from the smoldering coals played across his forbidding expression.

"Reckon we'll have any trouble crossing the Red this year?" Instantly Tate regretted his idle comment. Crossing the Red meant entering the Indian Territory.

Neely took a long drag. Blowing the smoke skyward, he said, his voice grim enough to chill the air, "We covered twelve miles today. At this rate we'll be crossing devil's land afore you know it. Ain't goin' be no trouble we can't take care of."

Tate untied the strings of his flour sack apron, the unspoken signal he was through for the day. He left Neely Wade by the fire as he prepared to bed down. Shortly afterwards Neely followed suit.

No sooner had he settled in, the trail boss, called Boss by all, appeared at his side. Having learned the trail by trial and error, Boss, respected by the trail hands, wrangler, cook, and Neely Wade, his *segunda*, shuffled his boots.

He spoke urgently. "Neely, you awake? Come on over here where we can talk."

Neely threw back the blanket, stomped on his boots, and grabbed his battered hat. Beyond the hearing of herd trail hands catching shut-eye he waited for Boss to build a smoke. It wasn't like Boss to disturb a man's sleep, Neely Wade thought. Today's peaceful drive with plenty of clear water creeks left him wondering what could be wrong. In the moonlight he could see Boss's furrowed brow.

"Won't be too long afore we pass east of Decatur village," Boss said, his voice tobacco-toughened. "That is if'n we don't take a long time on Elizabeth Creek."

Neely Wade nodded, thinking Boss, compact and muscular, was put together like a Steel-Dust bred horse.

Not sure where the conversation was going, he commented, "The new wrangler is workin' out pretty good."

Boss glanced at the Big Dipper before turning his attention back to Neely. "He ain't nothing but a kid dreamin' of being a drover."

"That's true," Neely agreed.

Boss started, hesitated, and plunged forward. "I got me a bad feeling. Something I can't hardly put my finger on. It's like I'm headed for the end of the trail."

Neely didn't know what to make of Boss's discouragement. He was always one to dally his tongue when it came to his worries. "Probably no worse than last year. Leastways we ain't pointed to Abilene. Bob-wire and bib overalls has about taken over."

Boss whistled air through clenched teeth. Checking the Big Dipper again, he said, "Better let you git some sleep."

Neely turned to leave; Boss called him back. "Don't say nothing about my misgivings," he said, embarrassed. "Reckon it was foolish talk."

Neely cocked his hip and hooked a thumb on his belt. His penetrating green eyes examined Boss's square face. "To my way of thinking we'll both play out afore the Chisholm does."

Boss laughed. "Night, Neely Wade."

Back in the bedroll, he went over Boss's concerns. Kansas troubles were nothing compared to his hatred of crossing the Indian Territory. He'd given his youth to a little Mexican tart, but his heart had gone to Laurie. Turning sideways, he cradled his head in his arm. The blood in his veins ran cold at the thought of Comanches. He could kill them all.

Chapter Six

P inned in his arms the trapped wildcat bared her teeth. She took a powerful bite on the firm hand gripping her arm. The metallic taste of blood smeared her tongue. Raking a free hand across her mouth, she spit on the ground. "You should not have done that!"

He clasped her shoulders.

Both hands on the gun, she stepped back. "Go back to the reservation. I do not want to shoot you."

"I like to visit in Texas."

Elena's knees quaked.

Nakiguaht eyed the gun.

Her grip tightened. "How did you happen upon the ranch of Doctor Farrar's?"

Nakiguaht looked aside, his voice deepened. "I was seeking medicine for Fox Eye."

"Medicine? Who is Fox Eye?"

Chin lifted, he proudly stated, "Fox Eye is my father."

"Why didn't you tell Doctor Farrar this? I could have spoken for you. He would have helped you. One time he took a bullet out of a Kiowa. Skin does not matter to him. What is his sickness?"

Nakiguaht refused to answer. Instead an eager glint flashed in his eyes. "Did you steal the black?"

Bristling with indignation, she boldly gazed at him. "I have a bill of sales. Doctor Farrar wrote it out himself."

"Where are you going?" The rasp in his voice was back.

"None of your business," she stated, alarm building.

"There are dangers on the trail," he said.

"There are dangers for a Comanche off the reservation," she reminded him.

Thumbing his chest, he gave her a pitiful expression. "You would shoot me?"

Braver than she felt, she waved the gun at him. "I may have to if you do not leave."

"But I wanted to thank the Mexican for saving a Comanche from hanging."

She cocked the hammer. The click sent an unmistakable signal. Tramping backwards for the sorrel, she watched his every move. When she handed over the reins fingertips brushed. Nakiguaht's lips twitched. Face pinched tight, Elena jerked her hand clear.

From the windward side of Ornery, he quietly mounted. Elena kept the gun on him. Soundlessly he vanished through the trees.

Puff.

Gone.

Breath solidified in her throat. Nerves at full stretch, she pressed her fingertips to her temples. *He wanted medicine for his father? The doctor was not there. I did not see a horse. He was stealing the black to escape. Any Indian off the reservation would be shot. He took a chance of being discovered. Yet he did not forsake the mare. I do not understand. But how did he find me? Doctor Farrar said the Comanche were clever. Pretending deafness saved him at the jail. Now he is following me. He still wants Ornery. I know it. Well, he cannot have him! He cannot have me either.*

She caught herself glancing uneasily over her shoulder. *Where is he?* Nauseating spurts of adrenaline coursed through her veins. For the third time she rinsed out her mouth even though the taste of his blood had since disappeared. *Mary Mother of God and all the Saints keep me safe and help me find papa.*

Gathering up her things, she dragged them closer to the horse. She sat cross-legged next to the animal with the woolen blanket wrapped around her shoulders, gun fisted in her hand. All the while the sensation of a spider crawled up her spine.

The night stretched on and on. Senses honed magnified the breeze rustling leaves. Night critters on the prowl sounded like moccasins softly padding close by. At first light, body stiffening in apprehension, she fully expected the savage to appear from behind a tree. To be sure, gun in hand, she policed the area. The thin stream gurgled peacefully. The region appeared undisturbed. *He is gone.* She hesitated to guess how far. There was no trust in her heart for him.

She took to whispering to the dog as if the heavens beyond could hear. "León, today we will find the Chisholm Trail, but not before I remedy the Nancy-boy taunt. I do not wish to be taken for a sissy boy. I will fix myself to look tougher."

Hidden in the trees bordering the stream she removed her shirt and began wrapping her torso with the red sash. At the most feminine part of her body she tugged as tightly as she could. Quickly, she slipped on the shirt and tucked the tail inside the tan trousers. To disguise her smooth complexion, she smeared mud on her face and under her nails. For an extra touch she practiced walking in the manner of the soldiers, longer strides, chin thrust forward.

The floppy hat of grain held up to Ornery, left over ham stuck in a biscuit for her and one for León completed the morning meal.

She found a handy stump to stand on which helped in tacking the horse and tying on the blanket roll. A full canteen and the grain sack hung from the saddle horn. She made sure the Army Issue Colt walnut grips were easily accessible from the sack. Mounted, she leaned over the horse's neck. "Thank you, Ornery. If *my friend*"—jaws tightened at the thought—"was around you would let me know." Even so she left the area with an uneasy feeling.

She followed the road to Decatur and at a slow walk entered the wide main street. Dogs barked at León; a crowing rooster perched on a water trough eyed the skies. In front of a store a clerk sweeping the boardwalk paused to watch. She passed a livery, a salon, and a hotel before checking up in front of a general mercantile establishment.

Behind the counter the storekeeper, a one-armed man wearing a frayed gray cap, perked up with curiosity. His straggly red mustache, doused with a large helping of gray, twitched. "Can I help you, sonny?" he asked.

Dust covered, floppy hat pulled down to her ears, Elena coughed. She pointed to a box of cartridges on the shelf.

A meddlesome old-timer moored to a nail keg had a glint in his eye. "Whar ya headed?"

She coughed again.

After paying for the cartridges, she counted her change and started for the door. She had her hand on the knob. "Sonny, be careful," the one-armed man called out.

Without turning around, she nodded, fully confident she could take care of herself. León, nose to the ground, raced around in circles in the middle of the road. Ornery, hip shot, wore an expression of a patient saint. Elena paid no attention to the pair of unsavory characters riding past except to notice they looked back at Ornery. Proud of her purchase of such a fine animal, she couldn't help but smile to herself.

Headed east of the village, Elena took note of the peaceful fenced ranches stocked with cattle. Pacing steadily, she scanned the terrain. After crossing a rock-bottomed creek, she emerged from a stand of trees. Deep ruts up ahead at the fork bearing north marked the trail just like Sergeant Powers had described. On the horizon, a slow moving cloud of yellow dust, a sure sign of a herd, caused her to blink, blink again, as her whole being filled with joy and anticipation.

Papa's cattle drive! Papa, my own papa! Her heart brimmed with overwhelming passion undimmed by the years, unfazed by haunting doubts. Soon she would see him. The unanswered love burning deep inside came forward with a rush.

Pulled by desire created by the sight of a herd, she spontaneously burst into a lope. Tongue lolling to the side, León raced to keep up. Common sense took over. It might not be *his* cattle drive, she told herself. In any case, the herd appeared miles away.

The westward descending fiery ball of orange was hard to deny. Now was the time to find a camp site. Tonight she'd build a fire and have coffee and bacon. Early morning she'd catch up with the herd.

All was right with her world until riders coming up on her backside materialized out of nowhere. The last passing had been a wagon load of hay pulled by a pair of oxen and driven by a young couple. She'd handled the lines while he'd walked beside the creaking wagon, a coiled bull whip held to his side. At the time the sun was directly overhead. Now the sky cascaded in sunset colors of lavender, pink, and bright yellow.

A chill passed over her. Elena glanced from side to side, frantic for cover. What she saw was the flat vastness of the north Texas prairie, grass weaving in the wind with the smothering smell of cattle hovering. She kept her little finger in contact with the walnut grips poking out from the feed sack.

The riders, two of them, were fast approaching. Too scared to turn around to look, she inched her free hand up the reins for a tighter control. Outrunning would be her only chance. In a surprise move they pulled up. The snorting and blowing of the mounts covered the discussion between them.

At the sound of hair-raising yells amongst pounding hooves, Elena kicked Ornery into a full gallop. The pair caught up. At Ornery's rump they split, hemming Ornery between them. A beefy hand reached out, grabbed her by the waist, lifted her from the saddle, and threw her off to the side. His pard grabbed Ornery's bridle and the pair made their escape taking her horse and all of the supplies with them.

She sailed through the air. The canteen shoulder strap separated from her body and rolled on the grass. She landed on a flat rock. Excruciating pain generated at her hip and radiated throughout her body. Shifting onto the hard, cattle-tramped earth she feebly concentrated on how to gather her limbs together. She wasn't sure she could.

León pressed his wet nose against her ear. Grabbing on to the dog, she pulled herself up. Squinting at the shadowy object in the weeds, she managed in a hoarse whisper, "León, help me."

Supported by her hand on his back she crawled to the dented canteen. Clutching the flask, she wormed her way behind a yucca plant and eased down in a dip in the earth. Like a cradle, she leaned back. Reaching inside her shirt, she loosened the binding red sash and breathed easier. She took a deep swallow and offered the dog a partial floppy hatful.

If I had camped sooner this would not have happened, she agonized. *I should have been more alert.* She could still feel the outlaw's beefy hand on her body. Fighting tears, she hugged the dog fiercely.

"Those sons of Satan stole Ornery, stole my horse, León, and all of our food. I have no weapon. We must not be afraid. We dare not think of wolves, snakes and…and" – she swallowed hard – "renegade Comanches. Tomorrow we will walk to the community called Nina. Sergeant Powers said we would pass such a place."

It was then she remembered the coins from the cartridge purchase were in the saddlebag. "León, I cannot buy food in Nina. What am I to do?"

***

Nakiguaht yearned to stay the night with her. Like a

mouse in the jaws of a rattler, the fear of him was upon her. Knowing she did not want him spiraled his spirits downward to the depths of his soul, but now that he'd found her, he'd protect the vision of beauty with his life. Most of all he wanted her to know he could never harm her. Silently, he disappeared from the campsite with a heart full of anguish.

Camped beside an obscure creek, he helped himself to the provisions confiscated from his escorts, drank from the refreshing water, and secured Farrar's horse out of sight. Among the cottonwoods he rested against the thickest trunk. Sunlight filtering through the leaves made patterns on his hands. One, he fancied, resembled a wolf paw.

He'd heard stories of Quanah Parker's father, Peta Nocona, the great Comanche warrior, never having been with another woman after his beloved wife, Cynthia Ann Parker, was captured and returned to her people. Until now, he had never understood.

His mind turned back to Chief Quanah Parker. Mow-way would have been his choice to lead the band. In a dry gulch he'd stabbed a grizzly bear to death. Now he wore a bear claw tied to his scalp lock, but Mow-way had given up. He had moved his family south of Fort Sill to spend out his days.

Quanah deals with white eyes. His three wives and many children do not cry in hunger. He did not want many wives, only one. Holding the magic of Elena close to his heart, he slept and dreamed the dreams of a man in love until night birds quarreling in the trees nudged him awake.

Dodging in and out of cover, he headed back to Elena's campsite to pick up her trail. After skirting Decatur, and by moonlight, the lone Comanche on a sorrel found dog and pony tracks pointed toward the Chisholm.

Out of nowhere traces of two horses appeared on the trail. He scanned the area until he picked out a joining feeder trail. Satisfied, he moved on. The two horses had made a sliding stop, followed by lengthening strides.

Leading Farrar's horse and in a squat, he lightly ran his hand over the indentations. The horses had separated and had come up on either side of Elena. Three horses, side-by-side, Elena's in the middle, had taken off in a full gallop. Impressions of the dog paws ceased.

Even by the sketchy moonlight, the spot Elena's body had landed was obvious. Her scuffed shoe prints, one dragging behind the other, disappeared in a sea of grass. Silhouetted against the silvery skyline, the tall plant caught his attention and, with the stealth of a stalking wolf, he eased toward the dagger-fingered evergreen. A dog growled. He smiled. Parting the plant leaves, he looked down upon Elena clutching the animal.

He rasped, "*Mi amigo.*"

The blood drained from her face. She could not run; she did not have a weapon. In a panic she grabbed the dog by the neck and scrunched behind his shaggy body. Wild-eyed, she peered between León's pointy ears.

Grinning, Nakiguaht rounded the plant, made his way down the recession and joined her. "I have come to visit."

The feel of a cold fist clamped over her heart.

"What has happened? Where is your horse?" he asked.

Nakiguaht waited. Minutes passed. "Tell me," he encouraged, moving closer. "I will not harm you."

León thumped his tail against her leg. Fearful images built in her mind. Slowly, she groped behind her back hoping to grasp a rock. She found nothing.

He asked again. "Where is your horse?"

She stared at his powerful chest. His stance emphasized the thickness and strength of his body. Her breath quickened. She remained mute.

Not to be denied an answer, Nakiguaht demanded,

"You must tell me."

She knew she had to speak. He was Comanche and he could get ugly. She had no defense. She prayed for a strong voice. "I... I... they stole my horse. The dirty, nasty desperado yanked me off and threw me to the ground. My horse...all my things...are gone." Gathering momentum, she declared, "There is no horse here for you to steal."

Nakiguaht started to reply, changed his mind and went to the sorrel. From the saddlebag he procured a coffee pot, coffee, frying pan, slab of bacon and hard biscuits. He laid them beside Elena's worn shoe tips. Blade flashing, he gouged the earth in the form of a pit.

León licked his hand. "Shuh, dog," he grunted, shoving him aside. Looking up at Elena, he said, "We eat before we decide what to do."

"We?" Elena gulped.

He did not answer. Instead, he chanted softly to himself.

Elena could not keep her eyes off him. Balanced on his toes, heels above the ground, he looked ready to spring. Quick movements of the knife blade flashed. Dread took hold, but he appeared more interested in the fire pit than her. Gaining a shred of hope for her life, Elena offered her canteen for coffee. Nakiguaht shook the sloshing contents and gave her a fetching smile.

The slow-burning fire, cow chips low in the pit, at last rendered a meal Elena devoured. Grease dripped off her chin. León wolfed scraps. She felt the gaze of Nakiguaht upon her. Curious, she glanced up and saw the pure enjoyment on his face as he watched her take her fill. Pretending not to be affected by the warmth starting at her neck and spreading upwards covering her cheeks, she rubbed her hands down the sides of her tan trousers.

"Now you must tell me. How did you find me?"

Nakiguaht handed her a tin cup of steaming coffee. "I followed your trail."

"You are following me?" Old fears returned with a vengeance.

"I am on my way to Cache Creek. A horse traveling with a dog is not hard to track." He positioned himself closer. "What are you going to do?"

To her dismay, her voice broke. "There is a settlement up ahead called Nina."

"It is a long walk," he said.

Elena bit her lip. She did not want to become discouraged. Tracing her finger round León's ear, she said, "It was brave of you to leave the reservation to seek Doctor Farrar's help. What is your papa's sickness?"

"Fox Eye is dying."

Nervously, she scratched behind León's ear.

"Nakiguaht means without ear," he baited.

"What happened?" she asked innocently.

Nakiguaht rose from the ground and stood with his back to her. Suddenly, he swooped in a crouch and faced her. Slowly, he lifted the left braid exposing a horrendous scar giving her full benefit of the wound in the firelight.

Elena sucked in; she drew back.

He tripped his fingers up his arm when he spoke of the wolf's ability to travel smoothly and silently in search of prey, his injured pony. Making claw like motions, he became the wolf nipping the leg.

Nakiguaht paused; Elena edged forward.

He whipped out an imaginary knife. Acting out the melee of the wolf ripping off his ear and the stab to the wolf's heart, he then crumpled to the ground. Whimpering, the dog licked his face.

Elena covered her mouth to stifle giggles. Nakiguaht stared at her and then burst out laughing. Coming to her senses, Elena gained composure and re-set the blockade of fear separating them.

Crestfallen, Nakiguaht frowned. "You are alone."

"I have not always been alone," she said, becoming

testy. "I had Alita at Fort Richardson."

"Who is Alita?" he asked.

She began fiddling with the corner of the red cloth hanging out from under her shirt. Her voice became thick and hard to understand. He edged closer.

"Alita was my cousin. We were together at Fort Richardson. The laundress work is hard. Now she is buried there with no one to visit her grave."

Nakiguaht pulled the knife from the leather sheaf attached to his belt. Elena eyed the feather dangling from the handle. Nakiguaht began plucking clumps of prairie soil. "I do not go to the graves of the dead."

"You do not respect the departed?" Elena challenged.

Nakiguaht grunted. "I am not afraid of the ghost images walking the graves by night unable to pass into paradise. The places of the dead are not healthy. They bring bad luck," he said as if she should know.

Ghost images? Walking the graves by night? "Graves cannot bring bad luck, but let us not talk of them."

"What magic do you wear about your neck?"

"It is a cross to remind me to pray to the Virgin Mary."

"Holy Mother of God," he chanted.

"How did you know?"

"Fox Eye took Mexican captives and that is what they said day and night."

Elena inched into the embankment. She drew her knees to her chest. The dog moved with her. All the unsteady camaraderie gained by congenial conversation vanished. She could not hide the dread in her movements or the apprehension in her eyes. Minutes passed before he spoke again.

"When the sun rises I will steal back your horse."

"That is impossible! Ornery will act up and give you away."

"Then I will teach you the Comanche way of taking back your horse."

Elena had to digest this. It was a tempting thought. The more she contemplated getting back the means of finding her father the more appealing the idea became. So intent on the possibilities she was barely aware Nakiguaht had disappeared until he materialized beside her. Handing her a blanket, he said, "Sleep. We leave when the sun greets the sky."

Cautiously, she accepted the covering. *I am no fool*, she thought, getting down to the facts. *He wants me to steal the horse for him. I can get close to the horse; he cannot. He needs me.* "It is dangerous to trail horse thieves in the daylight. What if someone sees you?"

Nakiguaht shrugged; Elena blinked and he was gone. She folded the blanket lengthwise, lifted the top half and pulled the edge over her shoulder. Part of her body touched the soft prairie soil. The times she'd slept outside when Alita was with Freedom, her husband, came to mind. The ground beside the tent was hard and unforgiving.

Deep in the heart of the North Texas prairie, she gazed at the stars twinkling and came to grips with a plan. *He will not harm me until he gets the horse. I will let Nakiguaht show me.* Stories of Comanche horse stealing had been legendary around Fort Richardson. It would serve the low down hard cases right. *When Ornery is safe in my hands, I will deal with Nakiguaht.*

Night breezes whispering through the dagger-fingered plant sounded like a Comanche calling her name. For a second, she mistook a night critter scudding by for moccasins on the prowl. Raised up on her elbows, she shifted her hip. Not more than a squirrel's breath from her lay Nakiguaht. Arm slung over his eyes, he spoke more to the twinkling stars than to her.

"Nakiguaht will not harm the beauty beside him."

Rigid, wide-eyed Elena prayed he was telling the

truth. *I must not be afraid.* "How is it you know my language?"

"Fox Eye had many Mexican captives. Luis was my age. We played many games together. He taught me."

"Where is Luis now?"

"Fox Eye traded him."

"Oh?" she said, trying hard to sound nonchalant. "Do you know English?"

"Some."

"Speak it."

The curses heard at Fort Richardson poured from his mouth.

"Those words are not nice."

"The white man is not nice. I do not like his language."

"Are those the only words you know?"

He did not answer.

An hour before dawn Elena was still wide awake. She side-glanced Nakiguaht. He appeared to be deep in slumber, the escort's rifle by his side. Second thoughts crept in. The more she contemplated stealing back her horse, the more uncertainty set in. Too many things could happen. *I must find my papa. I have to get to Red Station.*

Now is my chance. She raised her head, glanced from side-to-side until she pinpointed the horse's location. Silently, she rolled from under the blanket. Crab-wise she crawled closer and closer towards the horse. At a safe distance she stood, grabbed her hip, ignoring the pain. Stumbling, she reached the sorrel, unbuckled the hobbles and drew the bridle reins over its head. Hand on the withers, she attempted to mount.

First the crown, the scalp lock, and then the eyes, black eyes, that bored through her rose from the far side of the horse. Moonlight silver tipped the otter-covered braids. The rifle barrel glinted. Elena quivered.

Nakiguaht edged around the animal. "Why is it you

steal my horse?" he questioned, a trace of hurt in his voice.

Caught in the act, Elena croaked, "It is not your horse. It is the property of Doctor Farrar."

"It is a loan. He said so himself. When we greet the day we will take back yours."

His threatening stance plucked the nerve of escape. The firm grip on her arm steered her back to the blanket. León had found comfort there. Elena shoved him in the direction of the Indian's place as a barrier. She distinctively heard Nakiguaht snort "humph."

"Why are you on the trail? You have not told me."

Leaning over the dog's back, Elena's eyes narrowed. Facing him, but not looking directly at him, she watched to see what he might try.

"Tell me," he repeated with quiet emphasis.

"There is a herd on the way with my papa. I will be safe with him. It is better to stay here than try for Nina. I will walk out to the passing herds. I will find him. If I do not, he will come looking. He can track a flea on a mound of rocks." There, she thought, that will give him something to think about.

Plagued by doubts and the risks of her plan, Nakiguaht pondered the chances she'd have of success. *She has shown courage traveling this far on her own. Here there is no water and no food. It might be days before his herd arrives.* A long time passed before he answered. "You will need the black."

Chapter Seven

Nakiguaht tapped her shoulder. Elena came forward like she'd been shot. His face in hers, she spied a mole above his lip. Something she hadn't noticed before. Nakiguaht moved a fraction closer. She jumped up, grabbed her hip and collapsed in a heap. Nakiguaht offered his hand. "You fall like a wounded deer."

Refusing the offer, Elena rose awkwardly. Rebuffed, Nakiguaht stepped aside. "The thieves will be easy to track," he said, hiding the slight in his voice. "One rides a horse with a chipped shoe. We leave now."

Elena shielded her eyes checking the trail. No sign of cattle on the move. She looked to Nakiguaht knowing he was right. Her horse was necessary. She waited for him to adjust the saddle bag; fingers lingered over the confiscated rifle in the scabbard. Temptation flickered. As if reading her mind, he clasped his hand over hers and moved it away from the tantalizing bait. His action accompanied by a firm grunt left no doubt she didn't have a chance. Astride the horse, he indicated she ride in front.

The orange streaks in the silver sky promised a clear morning. Objects could be sharply defined for a mile or more. Easy prey, thought Elena. Nakiguaht leaned to the side studying the trail. She focused between the sorrel's ears. *He is Comanche* rang in hers.

At first she ignored the otter fur tickling her cheek, but the persistency of the sultry contact soon got the best of her. He was goading her, she knew it. Twisting in the saddle, she slapped the braid behind his shoulder. "There," she said. "Keep them to yourself."

Taking her hand in his, he said, "Otter fur is soft. It is like the wing of a butterfly."

"Nakiguaht," she blurted, yanking her hand free. "Take your games someplace else."

Elena heard his sigh as he guided the sorrel off the

cattle trail, slid from the horse and landed with a soft thud. From a crouch he hissed, "Go. Riders behind you. A renegade with you is trouble."

Three dust-raising mounts were coming her way. Frantically, she looked down for Nakiguaht. All she saw was a whisper of movement behind a clump of weedy brush. Back flashes of the beefy hand, of sailing through the air and landing on the hard ground, pumped her heart in her ears. Reins gathered in a tight hold, she moved on as Nakiguaht had instructed. León sidled up to the sorrel. He gave a yap announcing his presence. "*Bueno,* León. They will see the rifle and think twice." She checked the saddle boot. "It is gone! Nakiguaht took it."

"Hello up ahead!"

Head tucked, jaws tight, she kept on.

"Hello up ahead! We're with the drive."

Magic words! She halted, turned and waited for the dust-covered trail hands to catch up. She heard the squatty one in the middle say it weren't nothing but a wet-eared kid. The slim one crossed his hands over the saddle horn. Leaning forward, he said, "We lost twelve head last night. I'm a-wondering if you've seen any sign?"

She said she hadn't and in a voice full of hope asked if a Neely Wade was with them.

"We ain't got nobody by that name," the slim one replied.

Elena sighed. "*Gracias,* I hope you find them."

Thankfully, the trio turned back. Elena urged the sorrel forward, but not before she heard the squatty one comment he'd a-sworn the kid'd been riding double. She continued on. Every now and again she glanced at the empty saddle boot. Each time, anger mixed with hurt escalated. They could have been outlaws, horse thieves, robbers, she fumed. When Nakiguaht's head popped from a tall stand of prickly pear she ignored him.

"Ho!" he called out, standing full height holding the

rifle by his side.

The rifle gave her pause. In a slow and deliberate manner, she walked the sorrel straight to him and stared at the gun. "I am glad you are safe. I was scared for my life."

Slowly he brought his lips together and lifted his chin. "Harm would not have come to you." He thrust the rifle in front of him. "I had this trained on them."

Elena could feel the heat rise to her face. Nakiguaht mounted, took the reins and resumed trailing the chipped horse shoe, his hot, angry breath on her neck. She refused to complain or ask foolish questions. Instead, she alternated between studying the sorrel's withers and looking ahead at the silver-tipped grass and the creek up ahead. Smelling water, León and the sorrel picked up the pace. Nakiguaht guided the horse away from the muddy bank left by cattle crossings and followed the curve of the creek a fair distance.

Avoiding his wounded expression, Elena broke the silence. "Do you think we will find Ornery?" Warily she glanced around. Nakiguaht spoke at last. "They have been here." Nakiguaht offered his hand. "Come, I will show you."

In a peace-making gesture Elena accepted. Very aware of her hand in his, she felt an uneasiness taking hold. Cautiously she disengaged herself. León needed a burr pulled out from his thick fur.

He pointed out the horse droppings and the broken low-lying tree branch. "They passed during the night," he said, "or the one riding the horse with the bad shoe would have seen this limb. They are close by."

"How do you know?"

"There is no camp sign. They were close enough to make it to their hide-out."

"But...but I do not see such a place."

He nodded in the direction past the broken limb.

"If you try to take back my horse, he will alert the

robbers. Doctor Farrar says," she paused, twisted the corner of her shirt, "he does not like Indians."

Nakiguaht's black eyes narrowed. "We have ponies who do not like the white man."

Elena wrung her hands. "What will you do?"

"First I will scout and then I will show you the Comanche way of taking him back."

He disappeared. Time passed slowly. *What is he up to? His ways are foreign to me. His moods rise and fall. I must not become too comfortable around him.* Images of the *bandidos* played around in her mind. Tangling with them could cost her life. *I would not get far on foot.* Still the urge to run loomed. Feeling trapped, she sat beside the creek chewing jerky. Before each bite she sniffed the black meat and scrunched her nose. Coffee was out of the question. He'd said no fire and she didn't argue.

I do not understand. Why is he doing this? He has a horse. Maybe he will not return. Surely his escape on the doctor's mount will not set well with Jack County. No doubt he left his escorts in who knows what condition.

With the horse, or without the horse, I will find my papa. I must. He will care for me and not be like Auntie Rosa and Uncle Manuel. She began dreaming of paternal kindness, his sorrow for the long separation and the confession he had thought she did not live. He will keep her close and never again let her have to fend for herself.

She masked her inner turmoil when it came to Nakiguaht. Her head swirled with doubts. *Since the night I ran him off with the Colt he has not forced himself upon me, only the tease with the otter fur covering his braids. It is the horse he is after,* she reminded herself, *or is he?* The hours dragged by. *I should have run. Now it is too late.* Full dark was upon her when a raspy voice jangled her nerves. Her breath quickened. "Is it time?"

Their eyes locked, but Nakiguaht did not answer. His actions spoke for him. He hid the provisions amongst a tangled growth of reedy grass. Next, he began to remove the saddle, glanced at Elena, changed his mind and tightened the cinch. He checked the security of the rifle and lariat. Astride, he kicked his foot free of the stirrup. Elena swung on behind him.

An owl arched the treetops. Feathers flapping softly, the bird of prey's sharp claws clutched an overhanging branch. Eyes immobile in the goggle-like face, the nocturnal creature swiveled its head from side to side. Three haunting hoots wafted the night air. Elena shivered.

She circled her arms around Nakiguaht's waist, heart pounding against the back of his deep, wide, muscular chest. Like a rock between them, the wooden cross gouged her breast. Taking an easy lope, she sensed he knew exactly where he was going. A rod behind the dog followed.

Crossing the moonlit prairie on an angle from the cattle trail, Elena experienced a rush of keenly intense energy. The swish, swish, swish of the hock high grass, the determined direction of Nakiguaht, brought on a surge of excitement she could hardly contain.

Nakiguaht reined up behind a hedge row mixed with stunted mesquites. The horse blew and stomped. Tree-roosting turkeys gobbled. Slipping his arm around his back, Nakiguaht urged Elena off the horse. She'd barely touched ground when he told her to wait, he'd be back.

Positioned between the mesquites Elena stared until the rump of the horse disappeared into inky blackness. The intensity of her vigilance magnified the panting and soft padding of the dog as he came by her side. She pulled him close. Wound tight, ready to spring, she waited for Nakiguaht's return.

Each passing second seemed an hour. Worry lines deepened in her face. A thousand scenes of disaster flashed through her mind. She must be loco out here on the prairie ready to go head on with a pair of horse thieves. Doubts piled upon doubts.

The rustle of soft grass, the smell of horse, and she jerked around to confront Nakiguaht on foot leading the sorrel along the edge of the mesquites. She jumped up and ran to him.

"Do not worry. I have found your horse." He placed his free hand at her waist.

Tripping backwards from the silent comfort of his touch, she asked in an unsteady voice, "What must I do?"

"The desperadoes play cards in a cabin. They drink firewater. Your horse is tied to a broken fence rail. He is saddled. Go to the horse and bring him back to me."

"Where will you be?"

"Hidden in trees, I will have the rifle."

Elena's hands covered her face.

Nakiguaht grinned. "Be bold like the Comanche."

Elena tugged her floppy hat to her ears and swung on behind him. They covered ground at a lope until they came upon the woods. Nakiguaht picked his way through the thicket. Sorrel secured, they crept toward an opening which exposed a view of the cabin. Nerves tight, heart pounding, Elena strained to hear every whispered word Nakiguaht spoke...go to the well...wait...then to the fence...stay in shadows...do not pass the window."

"My horse will scream when he sees you."

"I will be mounted. We ride out fast."

The crunching underbrush shattered her trigger-sharp nerves. At the undeniable panting, she expelled a deep breath. Nakiguaht took hold of the dog. Elena made the sign of a cross on her breast, kissed her thumb and lifted it towards the tree tops. In a crouch, she glanced over her shoulder. Nakiguaht was invisible in the black woods. She turned back and faced the course.

Stooped low, arms spread to the side, Elena ran to the well. Plastered to the side of the base of rough rock and mortar, Elena chanced a peek in the cabin window. The table lantern cast a red glow on the face of Beefy Hand.

The back of his pard hunkered in burnished gloom. At the sight of the devils from Hades eeriness passed over her.

She crawled to the broken fence by the side of the cabin. Ornery nickered. Two horses in the dilapidated barn answered. Shaky fingers checked the cinch and fumbled with the reins wrapped around the broken rail.

A door creaked. Footsteps shuffled towards her. Drawing herself up in a ball, she disappeared in Ornery's shadow. She held her breath while the thief relieved himself, groaned and moved away. An eternity passed before the door scraped shut behind him.

Elena gripped the reins and started back, her soles scarcely skimming the earth. Looking ahead, she could barely distinguish the outline of Nakiguaht on the sorrel. Ornery's throat rumbled. She covered the remaining distance and into the woods in a panic run.

Freed from Nakiguaht's restraining hold León bounded out from the cover barking. Whiffing the Comanche, Ornery screamed. He reared up in a lashing stand. Elena yanked on the reins, bringing the horse down. She hooked her toe in the stirrup and was swinging onto the saddle when the cabin door burst open.

Beefy Hand, six-shooter drawn, looked about wildly. Beside him his pard held up a lantern. Hackles raised, León turned toward the intruders. The snarling growl gave away his position. Elena hipped in the saddle in time to see a flash of gunfire, watch the dog pitched in the air and hear his yelp of pain as he hit the ground.

"*Nuhquitó! Nuhguitó! Nuhquitó!*" Nakiguaht yelled.

Elena didn't need a scout to translate his guttural language. She was leaving as fast as she could. Branches raked her face. Briars tore at her shirt sleeves. Sounds of deadly reports pierced her skull. A tree trunk scraped her leg. Ornery stumbled. At last she broke free of the woods. Tears of terror streaking down her face, Elena raced across the open prairie.

Chapter Eight

 U nsteady on firewater, the bow-legged desperado swung the lantern to the side of him. His nasty-eyed companion wobbled in a crouch and fired off two shots in the trees.

Nakiguaht judged the distance, gripped the reins between his teeth and pulled the rifle from the boot. Draped over the side of the horse, he angled his charge from the woods toward the cabin. From under the sorrel's neck he fired at the lantern. The flaming oil spattered the chest of the holder. Screaming in shock, he fell to the ground.

His companion stumbled backwards. Nakiguaht caught the *bandido* under the chin with the rifle butt, hoisted him upwards, held him long enough to see the terror on his face, and then watched his sprawling fall. Pulling hard on the reins, he leaned back in the saddle. The front hooves grabbed at the sky before returning to earth and landing on the culprit's leg. The bone crack pierced the night air.

Nakiguaht spun the horse and raced for the shaggy mass deep in the shadows. Without breaking stride, he thrust his body over the side of the sorrel and scooped up the dog. One-handed he slung the animal across the front of the saddle.

Underbrush crackled, small limbs snapped as he threaded through the woods. Breaking free onto the prairie, he strained for sight of Elena on the black. Only the faint pounding of her horse gave him direction. She was headed for the creek. The warm blood of the dog oozed on his hand. Wind blowing from the southeast chilled his taut body as he galloped across the wide prairie. Elena waited beside the stashed supplies. Ornery, covered in white foamy sweat, heaved.

Nakiguaht called out, "Come quick!"

Fisting the reins under Ornery's chin, she urged the

drained horse forward. Despite his spent condition, Ornery's facial muscles tensed. Elena hung on to the leathers. Eye on his adversary, Nakiguaht maneuvered downwind of the black. Limp in his arms, the dog whimpered.

"León! Is he—"

"Run! Take the sorrel."

At a fair distance Elena hobbled the horses. Automatically, she loosened the cinches before returning to Nakiguaht's side.

"Will… will he live?" she choked, feathering the side of León's massive head with her fingertips.

"I will feel his body for injury." Gently bracing his hands underneath the belly, Nakiguaht lifted the dog off the ground and then took away his support. Not surprisingly, León collapsed. Much like he'd handled the foal, he probed and poked. "The bullet passed through," he said, pointing to a gash. "There is firewater in the hiding place."

On her way to the stashed provisions Nakiguaht heard her stumble, fall and scramble in her haste to help. "If only we could see," Elena lamented, handing him Junior Foy's black bottle.

"The moon hides from us," he said, his voice soft.

Hovered over the dog, he pried open the jagged flesh and poured on the burning liquid. The pungent smell of whiskey wafted up from the wound. Right ear pressed to the dog's chest, he listened to a faint thump, thump, thump. Elena inched closer, her breath a whisper brushing his arm. Nakiguaht spoke in low tones. "The spirit of life has not walked away."

She thumbed the sign of the cross on her breast. "You must tell me what happened. I heard gunshots."

"They were drunk on firewater. I shot the lantern. The one holding it was burned. The sorrel stomped the leg of the *bandido* with the gun. I could not leave our friend behind to die."

On the pretense of having to examine the wound, he reached across her lap where she cradled the dog. He was close, so close.

Elena took an uneasy breath. "You took a dangerous action."

Playfully, he said, "It was a surprise attack."

Reaction setting in, she began to shake. Nakiguaht grasped her shoulder. "You were *teconiuap.*"

"Tec… tecon…"

"*Teconiuap* is how we say brave."

More harshly than she intended, she declared, "I can take care of myself."

Moon rays took this moment to sneak around a cloud and reflect the hurt in his eyes. Elena, confused, forced herself to look away. Purposely, she focused on the knoll at both horses, side-by-side. Maybe he will steal him tonight. Doctor Farrar said the Comanches were clever. She checked on the dog stretched out on a patch of soft grass. Without a word, she went to the horses. After unsaddling the sorrel, she placed her own rig close to Ornery.

Fighting to keep awake to guard Ornery, the means of finding her father, she twisted first one way and then another. Always, the worry of Nakiguaht's motives hung in the back of her mind. Gradually her body succumbed to its needs and blessed sleep took over.

He moved his bedding closer to Elena. Bending over her, he memorized her every feature highlighted by the silvery moonlight. *Soon I will be left behind. It is her father who will take her. He will keep her from hunger. He will give her presents. I have nothing. I am hung between the Comanche way and the road of the white man.*

Elena woke with a start. Hip shot, Ornery rested beside the sorrel. She didn't see Nakiguaht. Satisfied her horse was safe, she glanced in every direction until she spotted a mass of yellow fur by thick brush. Gulping dry air, she ran to him. León raised his head, thumped his tail.

She touched the crusted blood over the wound and felt his nose for fever. "I will bring you water," she told the dog, but when she headed for the creek León staggered behind her.

The fresh water was too tempting. In seconds the braid was undone, her head beneath the surface. Under the water she could hear León lapping. The cross about her neck floated before her nose. Without warning Nakiguaht burst through the surface like an Aztec war god rising from the sea. Freed from braids his ebony locks glistened in the sun. Ripples of water trickled down his bronzed muscular shoulders and broad chest.

Elena froze. What a scary sight. A naked Comanche! Even so she halfway wished he'd raise up a little bit higher. Shocked at such a thought, she fled in the direction of Ornery and the sorrel. The saddle boot was empty. When she looked at the creek again Nakiguaht had vanished.

If she had the Colt with one bullet in the chamber, even a laundry paddle, she'd feel safer. *Where is he? Did he have his clothes on?* Face flushed, she braced against a sturdy cottonwood and studied the ground for a sharp pointed stick, a rock, something for a weapon.

Fully dressed, Nakiguaht materialized from behind the tree. Elena almost came out of her skin. Nakiguaht laughed. "You jump like a frog on a hot skillet."

"You should not sneak up on people," she said, sharpness in her voice. The otter fur wrapping his braids and a blue feather tucked in the scalp lock framed an expression of somber dismay.

She had to take a deep breath before she spoke. "Where did you find the feather?"

"A blue jay left it for me beside my braid wraps."

Elena began to fidget with the brim of the floppy hat. Uncle Manuel had drilled it into her how the Comanches treated captives, only to be reinforced by the soldiers' tales of horror. *So far he has been helpful, but what does that prove? He's had chances to take my horse and has not. Does he want a captive too? He has said Fox Eye had many Mexicans. Is that what he has in mind to take me to Cache Creek?* She prayed for a passing herd, one with her papa.

She kept an eye on Nakiguaht as he moved the campsite farther down the creek curve. The wide blade of the knife beside his moccasin and the rifle propped against the tree made her nervous. In an uneasy manner, she approached him. "The thieves took my Colt. Lucky for me they did not disturb my blanket roll or the sack of grain."

Nakiguaht grunted. "This is the last of the provisions. My escort was generous."

León toppled by her side. Striving for a normal voice, she said, "You saved his life, Nakiguaht. I am forever grateful."

"What is grateful?"

"It means I am in debt for your kindness. Are the Comanches grateful?"

"We are the *Nermernah*," he began, his voice deep, guttural. "The People. My grandmother told me our spirit came from the magical mating of the animals. I see myself in the wolf."

His seriousness was not to be denied. "How is it that you see yourself in the wolf?"

"The wolf protects his family."

"You could have protected your family and asked for medicine at Doctor Farrar's."

His black-layered look was not lost on her. Elena moved on. The saddles and bridles came under her scrutiny. She pulled matted grass from the bits, yanked a thorny vine clinging to the cinch and wished for oil for the leathers her Uncle Manuel had kept in a jar.

Seated beneath a shady tree, she ran Alita's silver comb through her hair, braided it and pulled on the floppy hat. Using a stick, she scraped caked mud from her shoes. Tapping a toe, she glanced up at the darkening sky announcing the oncoming of rain. It was then she felt the earth rumble.

She ran down the creek curve, through the trees and onto the open prairie. She could hardly contain herself at the slow-moving cloud of yellow haze on the horizon. Drawing a deep breath, she turned to find Nakiguaht standing behind her.

"A herd is coming! I am riding out to meet them. I will come back for my dog. He is not strong enough to keep up. Tie him to a tree please."

Face glowing, she shielded her eyes and stared at the oncoming bawling, bleating herd. Tears of happiness hovered near the surface. And then she braced herself. *Please, Holy Mary let my papa be with them.* Gathering reins, she spoke rapidly. "Thank you for helping me. Perhaps we will meet again."

"I will find the beauty of Lost Creek." Her mind on the herd drawing closer and closer, the mention of Lost Creek did not register.

Chapter Nine

*e*lena tightened her grip. The time had come. Heart in her throat, she left the tree-lined creek behind, headed toward the trail and the sluggish advancing haze of yellow dust. She kept a swing rider in sight until he checked up, stood in the saddle and waved his hat to the ramrod.

Three riders coming on fast kept to the side of the cattle. They clearly had her in their sights. She pulled up and waited for them to join her.

Scarcely able to control a gasp of surprise, she stared at Dan Belcher, Toby, the Jacksboro blacksmith, and a stranger. They appeared to be ghosts from another time. A stride in front of Toby and the stranger, Dan checked up.

"I'm the captain of this here posse. Junior Foy was with us, but he lit out." He pointed to the stranger. "Russ here joined up with us. We've already gotten information on you from a skinny fella with the herd up ahead."

Elena knew he meant the drover looking for strays. She watched the suspicious curl at the corners of his mouth. She moistened dry lips.

His squinty eyes narrowed. "Yeah, the folks in Jack County can't sleep nights with a savage on the loose. We figured he'd be on the trail looking fer horses and scalps."

Toby sidled up beside Dan. "Doc Farrar said you bought his black and took his dog alookin' fer yore daddy."

Dan shot him a look of annoyance. "Gard Young is the boss of this herd. We've been riding with him waiting on you to show up. I can tell ya right now Neely Wade ain't here."

Elena felt the very life drain from her body. "He is...he is not?" she whispered, her eyes downcast.

Toby spoke up. "No, he ain't."

Limp in the saddle, Elena fought tears.

"What I want to know is where's the Comanche

you're ridin' with?" demanded Dan.

Elena jerked upright. Shock brought on tremors. "What... what do you mean?"

Dan glared. "It ain't no need to deny it. You was seen ridin' Farrar's sorrel. The very sorrel the Comanche took. The drover with the herd up ahead said he thought you was ridin' double. Then when you come up and asked about Neely Wade you was alone. Now, where is the red devil?"

Elena sucked in. Fear knotted inside her.

Dan took over. "Doc Farrar said you was on the trail lookin' for yer daddy. I say you hooked up with the Comanche. Tell us where he is. Ain't no sense in you gettin' yourself into a mess of trouble aidin' and abettin' a hostile off the reservation."

Elena stiffened. "I see no Comanche."

Dan's jaws tightened. "Lyin' ain't gonna help. How do you explain ridin' Doc Farrar's sorrel? The skinny fella described the horse perfect."

Panic escalating she diverted her attention to the cattle lumbering by. Two muleys and a one-eyed pinto longhorn, head to tail, drifted aside. An alert drover, coiled lariat in hand, loped toward them.

In split second reaction, Elena ran her horse between the strays and the herd. Separated from the drive the muleys and the longhorn milled around the Jacksboro trio. Trapped, Dan Belcher's paint reared out of control. Toby stayed on, but he had his hands full. The stranger's horse shied and dumped him. The outrider, cursing and whipping the lariat, raised a cloud of dust. The diversion was enough. Elena cut across the prairie in a full gallop.

She'd hardly hit stride when lightning sliced the sky. Thirty seconds later thunder rumbled. Rain deluged from the heavens above and the roar of two thousand beeves on the move shook the earth. She could not tell if she was being chased or not. Longhorns abreast rumbled past and veered off.

Headed in the direction of the creek at break-neck speed, she had to warn Nakiguaht a posse was after them. He would help her. He *had* to. They couldn't capture her. Not now, not when she'd come this far.

A cloud-to-ground bolt of fierce blue illuminated the vast, bleak prairie. She took her bearings. She glimpsed the stand of trees by the creek. A long, wide depression lay between. Ornery lost his footing in the slick, wet grass. Afraid the horse would slip, she dismounted and trudged forward holding tight to the reins. The sound of running cow horses amidst the thundering hooves brought on the fear of being trampled to death. They were close, so close.

Keep moving, she warned herself. Keep moving. On and on she plowed through the black downpour. Twice she fell to her knees. Ornery walked heavily beside her. Fading shouts and gunfire indicated the herd was turning on an angle back to the trail. Relief flooded her system. Tension eased.

Elena and the horse developed a rhythm, slosh, slosh, plod, plod, until her right foot sunk deep into a gopher burrow. Pitched forward, her body twisted and thudded in a splashing heap. Never releasing the reins, she pulled the black's head with her. Splay-legged, nose in her face, he snorted. Righting himself, the horse jerked her arm and wrenched the shoulder muscles. Reins slipped through her fingers. At the very end she grabbed a tight hold.

Jaws clenched, she tottered to a stand. The weight on the twisted ankle sent shots of hot fire throughout her body. Walking was too painful. She'd have to chance the slippery turf. Grit garnered, she toed the stirrup with her good foot and swung onto the horse. The injured ankle dangled outside the stirrup. The damaged shoulder tissues proved to be more than she could handle. Acute pain began to block out her peripheral vision. Losing consciousness, she leaned over the horse's neck.

***

Sometime during the night the storm had passed. The early morning air hung heavy with humidity and thick fog. Steam rose from Ornery's neck. A single rein dangling from the bridle touched the rain-soaked grass. Head drooped, the black dozed.

Disoriented, Elena hung over the saddle. The squeezing pressure of her high-topped shoe was like a vice. To remove the torture she'd have to dismount. Wondering how much longer she could stand it, she placed her hands on the pommel and pushed herself upright.

Her shirt and trousers, sodden and heavy, clung to her clammy body. The hat brim stuck to her forehead. The oppressive humidity bore down unmercifully. Visibility of less than a yard gave her no sense of location. It did not matter. She had to relieve the agony or she'd die. Eyes tightly squeezed, she tried different dismount positions offering the least amount of pain.

After a few moments of tottering in the saddle, she slid from the animal and crumpled to the ground. Vaguely a dog yipping tripped across the recesses of her mind. Ornery's throat rumble echoed. Dreamlike the padded pounding of his hooves faded away.

She raised her head just an inch. The milky, vaporous fog parted enough to reveal the outline of a crouched bronze-skinned savage. A knife blade flashed in his hand. Acting without forethought, she screamed.

***

Nakiguaht secured the whimpering dog. From the tallest branch of the lookout tree, he watched Elena cross the prairie to ask about her father. *The gathering storm will delay her return for the dog. She will come back for León.* He knew it and he would wait.

Admiring the stride of the black and the way she handled him, he could not stop the sinking feeling in his heart. *She will find her father. He will know her courage.*

Misery wrapped itself around him. The black clouds took on shapes of headless buffalos in a state of frenzy. He could smell the moisture contained within.

When Elena appeared to be nothing more than a dot on the horizon, he climbed down. Crouched against the tree trunk, his arm around the dog, he experienced a roiling turmoil within. *I feel the disappearing sickness of my father. She has the courage of a warrior, the warmth of the sun and the beauty of a vision. Neely Wade will prize such a daughter.*

Mind wandering, he remembered the first time he'd seen Elena and how he'd waited on the banks of Lost Creek at Fort Richardson for her to return. How she had captured a kernel in his heart that grew and grew and the restless discontent when she did not return.

He mulled over the sight of Elena in the jail. The bravery shown revealing the truth about the weapon. The way she stood beside him. Close, so close he could touch her arm. All the while León, tied to the tree, sat on his haunches howling like a *lobo*.

The brewing storm chilled the air. Nakiguaht began to look around for shelter. Soon the skies would open. As he poured the remaining brown liquid on the dog's wound, he thought of the escort with firewater on his breath. He was a stupid white eye, but the revenge of escape did little to bring satisfaction to his heavy, heavy heart.

Not until a brilliant blue spear stabbed the earth did he scramble for cover. The sack of provisions, the rifle in his arms, he ran to a lip overhanging the creek. After stashing the supplies, he went back and checked the sorrel, untied the dog and hunkered down under cover to watch the rain gore the creek like a thousand lances.

Wo-haws trembled the earth; the sorrel screamed in fright. Lurching forward, Nakiguaht listened for the location of the stampeding cattle. They were near, but they were not headed toward the creek. There was nothing he could do. Drawing on patience bred in him by Fox Eye, he made himself sit under the arrowhead-shaped overhang and believe Elena was safe.

Smelling of firewater the drenched dog crowded in beside him. Together they waited out the pelting, relentless rain. Black and steady, the constant pour seeped through the clay-earth until little streams formed and soaked his clothing. Toward morning fog rolled in. On a prowl, Nakiguaht stopped, listened, and identified the sound of a horse pawing. Knife unsheathed, he silently skulked through the haze. The dog ran ahead yipping.

The sound of a familiar throat rumbled. The still, heavy thick mist gave him no way to approach downwind. His very nearness was a danger to Elena. If the horse reared or bolted, she could be injured.

In a crouch he waited for a lift in the fog. Stooping lower to the ground, his arms pulled close to his body, he could make out the dog running in circles near the misty veiled legs of the horse. What he couldn't understand was Elena not talking to the dog. By the horse's reactions, she must know he was near.

A welcomed wisp of wind began to stir and gradually parted the curtain of fog. The scent of Nakiguaht wafted past Ornery's flared nostrils. It was enough. The horse squealed and took off through a cloud of vapor, reins wildly slapping his sides. Unable to resist adventure, the yipping dog followed his companion.

In leaping strides, he covered the short distance. On his knees he gently cradled Elena in his arms. "It is Nakiguaht."

She shivered. Her teeth clattered. Struggling to sit up, she displayed such pain in her eyes Nakiguaht became even more alarmed. Following her hand motions, he saw the problem. Proceeding slowly, yet deftly, he tugged off the offending, squeezing shoe.

Holding her close in his arms, the shoe in hand, he

carried her back to the creek. Not to his surprise, side-by-side, the sorrel, the black, reins dangling from the bridle, and the dog were peacefully at ease on the grassy knoll. Giving them a wide berth he placed the hurting Elena under the lookout tree.

Huddled beside her, he took her hand in his and gazed into her tormented green eyes. Her suffering brought on a deep concern which morphed into gentle tenderness. He wanted her before the hand of age was laid upon him.

León, tongue lolling, bounded toward them. Before Elena could react, the dog took his place atop her foot. Doubling up in pure agony, she cried out.

By the scruff of the neck, Nakiguaht pulled the dog away. "*Ueto,*" he muttered.

León did not go. Instead, he crawled on his belly to Elena's foot and nosed his body underneath as if she would protect him from the Comanche.

Nakiguaht was about to remove the dog again when Elena gritted in pain. "Do not... do not... He is like a pillow to my foot. He brings relief."

Nakiguaht shrugged. He started for the creek to fill the canteen for Elena, but in a weak voice she called him back. Returning to her side, he asked, "What do you want? I will get it for you."

She wrung her hands. "I have something to tell you."

Chapter Ten

T he excruciating pain made it hard to form words. She knew she had to try.

"What is it?" Nakiguaht repeated.

"There is a posse… posse from Jacksboro…"

Eyes narrowed, he thumbed his chest.

She tried to wag her head.

Gently he removed the floppy hat. The silver comb askew in the braid dangled precariously. Flutter-light, he eased it from the tangles and set the comb aside.

"The posse? It is not after me?"

Elena stared into his black, questioning eyes. Mustering strength, she managed, "… *after both of us.*"

Nakiguaht sat back on his heels. "Where is this posse? You must tell me."

The warmth of his hand on her shoulder seemed to draw the life out of her. Propped against the tree, she closed her eyes. The tree turned into a wonderful, secure breathing support. She snuggled against a warm, flat surface she couldn't identify. A branch curled around her shoulder and down her arm.

She blinked, shifted. Barely detectable, the wonderful magic tree slipped away. Confused, she looked up. Nakiguaht stood there with the corners of his mouth upturned. Unable to express her perplexity, she tilted her head. Something was not right. In any case, she had to get up.

"I… I need to go to the trees."

He offered his hand. "I will take you there. I will come back for you."

Before she could protest, he'd slipped his arm around her waist. Hoisting her to his hip, he rendered her helpless against his body. She quivered. The quiver turned into a squirm.

He lifted her higher on his hip, his arm circling

under her breasts. A tiny fist blasted his shoulder. Legs went flying.

Nakiguaht tightened his grip. "I do not understand."

"You... you touched me! Put me down!" Her heel kicked his knee.

"You are like a wild cat." Nakiguaht held on.

A thicket of scrubby trees and tall grass offered the privacy she needed. Lips tight, she pointed in that direction.

"Do not point," he said, covering her hand with his.

She demanded, "Why not?"

"Your hand will wither away."

He was so adamant she twisted enough to see his eyes. Yes, she thought, he is serious. "Who says my hand will wither?"

"The Comanche."

The prideful declaration left no doubt. He meant it. Stumbling into the thicket, she palmed the nearest trunk for balance. Her head hurt. The throbbing made her dizzy. *What am I to do about Nakiguaht? At grave risk he did not forsake the mare. He rescued my horse. He saved my dog. Ghosts walking on graves, hands withering, wolf ancestors are not right. Holy Jesus and all the Saints! A Comanche.* She wished she'd never listened to the horror stories told at Fort Richardson or heard Widow Speer's wailing. *I must be careful. It is trust I do not have.*

She did not call to Nakiguaht like he had asked. She found a limb on the ground, improvised a crutch and emerged from the secluded copse on her own. Before she reached the lookout tree Nakiguaht appeared by her side. He did not offer help. She caught the sullen expression of someone who'd been slighted. *I have hurt him*, she thought with insightful clarity. *I did not ask for his help.*

She hopped along on her good foot, wondering if the crutch had been a mistake. The swelling round her ankle had increased. A tiny wince escaped. Nakiguaht pretended not to hear. His voice became serious. "The posse. You must tell me."

"Three men from Jacksboro, Dan Belcher, Toby, and another, Russ is his name. They want to capture you. Word has gotten to them by the cowhands looking for strays I was seen on the horse you ride, Doctor Farrar's sorrel. They figure we are together. I am wanted, too, for not telling your whereabouts. That is trouble for me for aiding and abetting a renegade."

Elena told how she'd escaped. "I had to warn you," she said, fingering the cross. "Then I tripped in the gopher burrow. In the fog I did not know you."

He waited patiently while she settled under the tree. After he handed her the canteen, he vanished. Dusk turned to darkness. The waning moon winked at her through the whispering leaves. Night spiders crawled on her naked foot. In pain she leaned forward and brushed them off.

She could see the black silhouetted against the moonlit knoll was alone. The sorrel was nowhere in sight. *The posse has scared him off.* She raked her arm across her nose. Tamping down her roiling feelings, she refused to dwell on being left behind. *He could have said good-bye.*

At daybreak I will mount up and continue on to Red Station. If drives pass me I will ask for my papa. The posse cannot take me. I have done nothing and the Comanche is gone. They will ask me where he is. I can tell them with an honest face, I do not know. She looked again at the knoll. A niggling of a puzzle nudged. *Nakiguaht did not steal my horse.*

"León," she called. "Come, León." No pants, yips or tail thumps could be heard. *My dog is gone, too! Nakiguaht has some nerve. Fleeing from the posse is one thing, but taking my dog with him is mean. He should not have done that.* Alone under the tree a wave of apprehension swept through her. An uneasy sleep followed.

The gray-pink sky of the dawning hour brought the twitters of morning birds. Despite the soreness and stiffness of her injuries and the night spent propped up against the tree. Elena knew it was up to her to take care of herself. It wasn't the first time.

Ornery neighed as she hopped past him on her way to the creek. At the bank she scooted out of her trousers, slipped off her shirt and slithered into the cool water. Towards the middle of the creek she ducked under, black hair fanning around her shoulders. She dove deeper until only her olive-skin bottom was above the water.

Floating on her back, she stared at the precious heavens above. "I can do it," she told herself with a splashing, kicking paddle. The motion brought a stinging to her injured foot. It was a good kind of stinging. The rotation of her shoulder as she tried to swim on her back proved to be too painful. She kept her arms to her side. Bobbing and weaving, the cross played around her chin.

When her hands shriveled Elena crawled out the water and dressed in the tan trousers and the army standard gray flannel shirt. The sash wrapped tight would only make her more miserable. Massaging the injured foot, she noted the swelling had gone down.

Chin jutted, hands fisted, she hopped back to the tree. Twice she tried bearing weight on both feet and found she could almost tolerate the pain. Seated under the lookout cottonwood, Elena fingered Alita's silver comb and for the first time did not think of her cousin in the cold, cold ground. The remembrance of the gentle way Nakiguaht had untangled the comb from her hair took precedence.

Angry and hurt, she began to fume. *He did not say where he was going and...and he took my dog. It was the posse he feared. He needed to escape, but he could have at least said so.* She yanked the comb through her hair. One stubborn knot tested her patience. Face screwed up, eyes tightly closed, she was about to lose control when a familiar voice behind her caused the comb to fly from her hand.

"I have something for you."

Elena swung around. Her heart skipped.

Keeping his hands behind him, Nakiguaht kneeled beside her. Slowly, he brought forth the bulging feed sack and sat it on her lap. Peeling apart the duck canvas handles, Elena was overcome by the undeniable smell of apple pie, the golden crust still intact. She looked up at him.

"There is more. Look and see."

The wondrous smell of pie and the cloth wrapped lump beneath brought on a swarm of gnats. Elena swatted them as she lifted the corner of the bleached feed sack. Fingernails dug into the corner of the bleached feed sack; she blinked at the smoked ham and the fresh supply of oats beneath the pie. She tried not to imagine how he might have gotten the sack of coffee.

Elena wore the look of fright.

Alarmed, Nakiguaht asked, "What is it?"

"Where did you get these things?"

"I took them from a generous rancher."

Elena faced him. His black eyes had all but disappeared behind hooded lids. "Where is this rancher?"

Nakiguaht snorted. "Safe in his bed."

Visibly her shoulders relaxed. Nakiguaht bristled. "Quanah says there will be no more bloodletting in Texas."

"Who is Quanah?"

"He is the band chief. Quanah is leading us down the white man's road, the same road of his mother."

"But… but you stole…" Her voice trailed off.

Nakiguaht growled. "The white eyes stole our land."

"The Comanche stole from the Mexicans," she reminded him.

Nakiguaht grinned. "We are even. Let us eat pie."

The tempting odor, hard to resist, wafted up from the feed sack. Gliding a fingertip across the crust, Elena said, "If the rancher knew you came in good faith, he would have given you these things."

They both laughed at her lie.

Coffee pot in hand, Nakiguaht began to fan the campfire to life. Elena limped to his side, worry creases on her brow. "The posse. They will see the smoke."

Nakiguaht sat on his heels. Carefully, he laid one end of a stick on the burgeoning flame.

"Nakiguaht! Did you not hear me?" she demanded.

Holding back laugher, he teasingly lifted the left otter covered braid. Vexed, she stared at him.

"Do not worry. The posse is ahead of us on the far side of the trail. They spent the night with the stampeded cattle."

"You took a chance, Nakiguaht."

Quite unexpectedly, he lifted her foot onto his lap and began to rub the swollen area with his wide thumb. The soothing motion set off a heated comfort she couldn't deny. *It is medicinal*, she told herself. *It is like Uncle Manuel rubbing down a horse with a sore leg.* The thought of protesting came to mind, but her vocal chords stalled. "Riding today will be difficult," she murmured.

"We leave tonight. Before this moon dies we will reach the red waters."

Elena smiled. "My place is with my papa. It is a miracle Doctor Farrar found him for me."

Nakiguaht grumped. "I do not have a place."

Surprised, Elena turned to him. "What do you mean? Tell me," she urged.

"The ways of the white man take over. There is no place for me."

His deep voice, full of anger and resentment, startled Elena. Hesitantly she offered, "You have the reservation."

Nakiguaht rose in a huff. Kicking the steaming dung of the sorrel, he growled, "That is what I think of the promises of the white man and the reservation."

Before she could reply Nakiguaht stalked off in the direction of the creek. Beside the bank he disappeared. Under the arrowhead-shaped ledge, Nakiguaht relived the night of the storm. He could hear the wo-haws stampeding and mourned for the buffalo. *The cattle of the white eyes are a poor excuse for sustenance. Fox Eye is dying from the denial of the hunt. Even his many ponies are gone.* He had no place. Soon Elena would find hers and he would not see her again. The thought rendered a deep-throated wailing chant of hopelessness and sorrow.

The chant quivered her flesh. The intonations, muted and sharp at the same time, conveyed such loneliness, strange and disquieting thoughts began to race through her mind. A fleeting desire to go to him passed through her, warmed her and then turned to despair. *He is suffering. He came to me when I was hurting and I should go to him.* Desire mixed with caution fluctuated between her heart and her mind. Stricken, she remained rooted to the ground.

Darkness coming on, Elena knew she had to get ready to ride. She stared at the battered footwear clutched in her hand. Dread mounted. She centered the shoe top over her toe. *My shoulder has healed. I could ride Ornery if I had the nerve to put on this shoe.* Gingerly, she touched her puffy ankle. At the thought of entrapping the soreness in the confinement of the stiff leather, she winced.

Nakiguaht loomed by her side. "Why do you take so long?"

"I need courage," she lamented. She held up the shoe. "This will squeeze my ankle. I will ride with my foot bare."

"That is not wise. You need protection from the stirrup."

Gritting her teeth, she placed the shoe top in position.

Before she could poke her toes inside Nakiguaht

had the shoe in his hand and his knife unsheathed. Her eyes widened.

"I will make slits in the side."

"No! You will ruin my shoe. It is my only pair."

Nakiguaht made the first cut. Elena jumped up. Hopping on one foot, she reached for the shoe. "No! No!"

Knife in one hand, shoe in the other, Nakiguaht wrapped his arms around her tottering body. She tried to snatch away the shoe. He held her steady. In a surprise move he let go of the knife and tickled her ribs.

"Do not do that," she pleaded, muffling a giggle. His fingertips danced up her spine. She couldn't stop her breathless titters. Helpless in his arms, she heard his quick intake of breath. More surprised than frightened, she looked up. His gaze wandered from her eyes to take in her full body bringing on an awareness of just how close he was to her. Too close. Fearful where this was leading, she shoved Nakiguaht backwards. It took both hands and all her strength.

As quickly as the playfulness had begun it ended. Elena dusted off her trousers and adjusted her floppy hat. Nakiguaht picked up the shoe and slashed another gash. After flexing the high top, he attempted to slip it on. Elena grabbed the shoe from him and put it on herself.

"You need moccasins," he grunted.

In a pool of darkness they prepared to mount up. Each gave the other a wide berth and pretended nothing had happened. Saddle over her arm, Elena approached her horse. Accidentally, she brushed against Nakiguaht in passing. In a quick move, ankle stinging, she hopped to the far side of Ornery.

The moon, hidden by clouds, failed to light the way. She had to depend on the sound of hoof beats and the occasional glimpse of a murky rump. Nakiguaht crossed the cattle trail and veered off in the direction of a stand of timbers.

They passed over a wide, flat area with bedding ground sign. She reined up, shook her foot out of the stirrup, and hooked her leg over the horn. She could hear the dog sniffing cow pies. Nakiguaht turned back and joined her.

"What is it?" he asked.

Elena tightened her hold on the reins to keep Ornery from bolting. "My foot makes my leg numb. I feel nothing."

"Can you ride?" Concern tinged his voice.

Elena nodded. She swung her leg back over the side of the horse and toed the stirrup. "Yes, let us go."

On and on they traveled. If they passed too close to mesquite trees, roosting wild turkeys gobbled. A sharp-shinned hawk peeled overhead. Across the rolling prairies and deep valleys, Elena kept her focus on the dark moving shape of the sorrel. The dog brought up the rear.

At a timber line Nakiguaht edged up to her side. Ornery stopped cold and tossed his mane. Elena reassured the antsy horse with the touch of her hand on his foam-flecked neck.

Nakiguaht nodded toward the thicket. "Follow close. The underbrush is thick. There is water."

Elena felt like she had entered a den of unknown horrors. Briars reached out and grabbed her legs. Limbs she couldn't see scraped her arms and face. Behind her she could hear León's pants.

Nakiguaht pulled up to a stream so black and still only the splash of a frog and the dog lapping revealed its presence. More drained than she cared to admit, she hunched over the saddle.

Dismounted, Nakiguaht secured the sorrel before approaching the black. Ornery's ears flattened. Elena felt his hooves rising. She wrapped her arms around his neck. Ornery twisted and nipped Nakiguaht's shoulder. He fisted the reins tight under the horse's chin and held him. Gently, one-handed he pulled Elena from the saddle. He waited for her to gain balance before he turned on the horse.

Nakiguaht spewed Comanche words.

Ornery fleered. The white of its eyes flashed.

Elena took a stance. Her voice sounded like low rolling thunder. "You better not hurt my horse."

Keeping the gelding under control, he hobbled him. Rounding his rump, he slapped it hard. Ornery gave a sideways cow-kick. Missing its target, Nakiguaht laughed.

Stumbling, Elena made her way to an umbrella-shaped tree, damp leaves banked at the base. Afraid of what critter might be hidden in the debris, she raked the mound aside with a brushy limb. Back against the tough bark, she shut her eyes. The padding of Nakiguaht's moccasins faded. *He's on the prowl, checking. Nakiguaht has patience*, she thought. *If a horse had baited Uncle Manuel he would have done worse. Uncle Manuel had a mean streak.*

León hit the water like a thunder burst. Elena could hear the splashing. When Nakiguaht returned she moved over to make room for him. "How did you know of this place?"

"It is an old trace."

Elena eased her fingertips inside the top of her shoe. Seeking relief, she pressed the swollen area. "I have lost my way. Where are we?"

"The stampeded herd is above us. They will cross the Red before the sun sets if the waters are not angry."

"The posse does not know where we are. They have not tried to find us."

"The posse is near."

"How do you know?"

"I know."

"You will be safe at Sill. You must tell the agent you left the reservation for medicine. He will understand."

He spewed Comanche mixed with curses common

to Fort Richardson. His mutterings even included an ugly comment in broken English. His guttural tone stirred the hair on the back of her neck.

Bounding in her lap, León buried his nose under her arm. Glad for the diversion, she scolded, "León, you smell terrible."

Nakiguaht snorted. "He smells like frog. Get sleep. We rest here."

Sleep, Elena thought. *How can I when I am so close to Red Station?* She glanced at Nakiguaht. His arms folded across his chest, legs outstretched and as far as she could tell his eyes were closed. She thought of the attack she'd had at Fort Richardson. It was late. To this day she was thankful for the laundry paddle she had with her. It was the best of the lot and she'd claimed it, protected it as her own. She was on her way to the bakery hoping Phillip had set aside a loaf in exchange for washing his shirts.

The foul-smelling soldier had materialized from behind the long shadows of the bakery. He'd pinned her against the wall still warm from the ovens. His hands tore at her clothes; he grabbed her bare breast. Twisting and turning did not prevent his groping under her skirt. Somehow, she'd managed to grip the laundry paddle with both hands. With all her strength she let him have it across the face.

In shock, he stepped back. Both hands covered the blood pouring from his nose and from under his eye. Freed, she ran like the demons of hell were licking her heels. The next morning she could not pass a trooper without looking for a battered face. She never saw one.

She glanced again at Nakiguaht. He is sleeping. I must rest for the night's ride. Scooting down from a sitting position, she wiggled till she was comfortable. Her weary bones, especially her foot, ached from the ride. Sleep did not come on gradually and before she knew it and under the cover of darkness they prepared to carry on.

Nakiguaht once again took the lead. Beyond the timber line, they faced a wide stretch of open prairie. The smooth gait of the black fairly skimmed the terrain. Elena, wind in her face, could hardly wait to reach her destination. *When the sun rises Red Station will be close.*

Chapter Eleven

T he upcoming cattle herd stirred and began to move off the bedding ground, but the trail hands wandering in were not replaced. Each and every one clutching their hats in respect ringed behind the *segunda*. Bareheaded, Neely Wade looked down upon the grave of Boss. A breeze lifted the ends of his long straggly hair. Tate 'Tater' Hagan, the cook, came forward to say a few words.

"He was a good man, Lord," he started, choking on his words. Unable to complete his thoughts, Tater stepped back.

Focusing on the fresh mound beside the trail and the wooden cross marking the grave, Neely Wade began the cowboy hymn in his trademark mournful voice.

> *There's goin' to be a great big roundup,*
> *When the cowboys like doggies will stand,*
> *Cut out by the Rider from heaven,*
> *Who'll be there and know every brand.*

"Boys," he said, his voice somber, "you know I'm in charge now. Boss would've wanted us to take this herd to Newton without losin' a single head and that's what we're goin' to do. We'll git the job done for Boss. We'll keep the same rotations of riders. I'll do double if I have to. Any questions?"

After an uneasy silence Tater spoke up. "We better git a move on. Coffee's ready."

Paired up in twos and threes, the hands shuffled behind Tater. Neely filled his cup and wandered off. Tater made a point not to come up on his blind side and handed Neely a tin plate of sourdough biscuits and bacon. "Ain't no need to scout ahead," Tater said. "I'll take the wagon to the nooning place we used last year. You'll find me."

Head downcast, Neely accepted the plate. When he looked up to acknowledge Tater's plan his eyes were muddied in turmoil. The cook backed off, gave a nod and returned to the wagon. Left alone he couldn't stop reliving the accident. Cattle lowing, horns clacking, horses neighing and saddles creaking, so much a part of his job, did not register. His mind suffered back-flashes of Boss's mangled body.

I should've shot that outlaw steer when it'd showed its colors, he brooded. *I don't know what startlement caused Boss's horse to throw 'em right in front of 'im. I seen it comin' and I jes couldn't get there fast enough. Boss should've rolled, moved and kept movin'. Bein' gored ain't a good way to go.*

Neely Wade grimaced and braced himself for the upheaval of another bloody scene, one that had brought on the hardening of his heart. Laurie. The Comanches, the smoke of the cabin burning, the wild screeching and he knew, no matter how hard he ran from the field, he'd be too late.

He'd had this exchange with himself before, the one that always began with *the Lord giveth and the Lord taketh away. The cholera took ma and pa. Then there was that Meskin bunch what fed me, clothed me, and taught me what I know about horses. They treated me kindly until Maria Lopez took a fancy to me. Only trouble was she took a fancy to every vaquero in sight.*

He felt his jaws tighten. The night the baby had been born, he'd gotten drunk as a coot. Maria cried out it was his. He'd never believed her. Later, he'd wondered if the baby had even lived. Maria didn't.

The bottom had fallen out the sky that night. Tucked under his old woolen coat, the newborn never moved. Rosa had to accept the unwanted bundle. Maria was her sister and she had no choice. Disgusted, Manuel had complained it wasn't a boy.

Me and Boss'd been up the trail three times together. We was close. Knowed each other's ways. Now he's gone. Slowly and painfully the tiny crack in the steel cage round his heart clicked shut. There would be no turning back. His lean, sinewy body tightened as he built another smoke.

Spurs jangling, hat pulled down to his eyes, Neely Wade gave a hand to Tate harnessing the team. When the chuck wagon pulled out he mounted up and joined the herd.

Chapter Twelve

C oming in the cottonwoods lining the stream and after the long ride, Elena noticed a trio of mesquites on the far side of the trail. For a fleeting moment, she thought she'd seen a giant three-leaf clover rising up out of the prairie.

Ornery and the sorrel heaved. León lapped the stream. Elena rubbed down the horse with a handful of grass. When Nakiguaht led the sorrel next to them Ornery swung his head to the side and bared his teeth.

Embarrassed, Elena said, "I wish this horse would behave."

Nakiguaht grunted.

Elena glanced over her shoulder. Nakiguaht, back to her, was running his hand down the front leg of the sorrel. "This horse should appreciate the risk you took to get his oats."

"Change is not easy," Nakiguaht stated.

The abruptness of his tone caused Elena to pause. "Maybe he thinks you are a Kiowa."

Nakiguaht gave her a blank look.

"Doctor Farrar said one night he was coming into Jacksboro and Ornery started acting up. He gave him his head. Ornery took him off the road, into the woods and out of the path of four Kiowas." She turned back to the horse. "Ornery," she teased, "Nakiguaht is Comanche, not Kiowa."

Nakiguaht dipped into the feed sack and offered the black a handful of grain. Ears pinned back, the horse muffled his palm. Elena looked surprised.

"He needs food. He will accept it from his enemy."

"One day you will be friends."

"The black is old. He will not change."

She pondered before she spoke. "Sometimes change is what you have to do."

Nakiguaht stalked off. *Change*, he thumped his chest, *is poison to the heart. Fox Eye, longing for the hunt, the raids, the ceremonial smoking and the freedom of the vast land claimed as their own now sits in the ruins. He will not accept the white eyes' ways. They remain his enemies.*

Some in the band take steps on the road of the white man. Sore-backed Horse camps on a creek near Fort Sill to stay out of trouble. He was chosen to help pick the ones to be sent to a far-off place by the iron horse. Soon a cabin was built for him. He does not like the cabin. He says heap snakes inside. He camps in the yard. Would Elena like a cabin? Again, he thumped his chest as if to beat out the notion. "Humph," he snorted.

Elena figured out Nakiguaht had two humphs, one bordering on laughter, the other, despair. This snort signaled despair and after a time she quietly followed him. In strained silence they dug a fire pit. Nakiguaht pulled a lacy-leafed limb over the flame to dissipate the ensuing smoke. When the coffee boiled Elena filled and handed him the tin cup.

"This is the last of the ham from the gracious rancher," she said, savoring each bite. "Tonight you will be safe in Indian Territory and I will be at Red Station."

"Then we will part," Nakiguaht said.

"I could not have made this journey without you. Tell me, Nakiguaht, what is it like on the reservation?"

Crouched beside her, he took her hand in his. With his fingertip he drew a line across her palm where the fingers attached. "This is the Red River. No one from the bands can cross it." He traced another line. "Cache Creek."

Tucking her chin, she stared at the strong, protective hand cradling hers. Hands that had saved the foal, rescued her horse and brought back her dog. If not for him, she would have died after the stampede. She cleared her throat pretending not to be affected by the fingertip tracing her palm.

He made a gentle stab. "Here is Fort Sill." Making a slight trace south, he located the Kiowa-Comanche Agency. Across her thumb he drew the Washita River. North of Fort Sill, he dotted the Wichita Agency at Anadarko.

"There is talk the Kiowa-Comanche Agency will be moved to Anadarko to join the Wichitas," he said.

"Is that a good move?" she asked, her voice soft.

Nakiguaht shrugged. He began tracing the patterns of arrowheads. "The agent tells us the land is better and there is more wood at Anadarko. The bluecoats and the agent argue about the move. They say it will cost the white father in Washington less money. Fox Eye says they want us further away from Texas. The land on Cache Creek is good for horses."

"Then I would stay on Cache Creek!" Elena declared.

Chortling, he squeezed her hand.

Continuing on, he began to frown. "The buffalo is gone. Rations keep us prisoners on the reservation." His frown disintegrated to a scowl. "The agent wants us to be farmers."

Leery of his escalated diatribe, Elena freed her hand. "On the reservation how is it you will explain the sorrel you ride? Will there be questions? You could explain it is a loan from Doctor Farrar. You went there for medicine. Escaping the escorts will be hard for them to accept. You could say you needed the medicine." She thought a second. "How did you get to Doctor Farrar's?"

"I rode my pony. I left him by the creek behind the ranch of the doctor."

Her mind flickered back to Dan Belcher's attitude. She remained quiet. He'd spit out a Comanche phrase as if he knew what she was thinking. When she'd first heard the language it scared her. Now the guttural sounds were so much a part of Nakiguaht and, for reasons she couldn't make herself accept, she'd gotten used to it. Her only regret was she didn't know what he was saying.

Slow at first, like the gathering of a storm in the far distance, the earth began to shake. Elena glanced around. Nakiguaht was standing by the sorrel. The black flattened its ears.

She jumped up and ran to the edge of the thicket. There she could see the herd cloud coming up on the clover-shaped clump of mesquites on the far side of the trail. She could hear the clacking of the horns, see the point rider, and taste the smell of cattle. Her heart raced. She hurried to Ornery.

"Cattle coming, cattle coming," she exclaimed. "I am riding out. My papa! My papa!"

In a flurry she tacked the horse. She found an old neckerchief in the blanket roll and laid it on the ground. Dumping out half the oats in the cloth, she chatted in rapid fire reports.

"You must not let anyone see you."

She tied the ends in a knot. "I will not give you away. If I find a doctor, I will ask for medicine for Fox Eye."

She offered him the bundle of oats. "Please be careful."

Lightning fast, he attached the saddle boot to her saddle. He shoved the rifle inside the leather sheath and shook the handle.

"Can you shoot this?" he asked.

"If I have to," she answered truthfully.

Ornery pranced sideways.

Elena looked down from the horse. Her heart gave a tug. If not for Nakiguaht she could not have made it. Still, the high trembling anxiety this may be her papa's herd took precedence. "Goodbye, my friend. May the angels watch over you"—her voice trailing off—"until you are safe."

Before Ornery had completed three strides,

Nakiguaht had tied on the remaining provisions, and was one horse length behind. Elena glanced over her shoulder.

"I will ride with you to the end of the thicket."

At the break in the trees Elena reined up and took a deep breath. Focused on the upcoming herd, she failed to notice the activity at the triple arrangement of mesquites. She could sense Nakiguaht behind her.

"Get back," he hollered.

Elena hipped around to stare at him. It was too late.

***

If it hadn't been for Russ, the J&R Ranch posthole digger waiting on a shipment of wire, with the posse, Dan Belcher would not have been behind the mesquites that looked to him like clubs on a deck of paste boards. After the stampede, Russ and Gard Young's wrangler had spent the night over-indulging in the cook's beans and the wrangler's supply of pecans. Dan had about had it with Russ's retching. He'd lost count of the times he'd dropped his britches.

Instead of riding out to join the upcoming herd to wait for the greaser, Dan, the captain, had no choice but to tarry for the cattle to pass. When the team of mules hauling a wagon rumbled by he waved to the driver. Toby wanted to know what they were going to do.

Dan said they'd stay put and wait. To pass the time, he suggested a friendly game of cards. Toby wanted to know the stakes. Squinty eyed Dan said with a sly glance at Russ he had a sack of pecans. Polite-like, he asked Russ if he wanted in.

Russ heaved, turned his back and gagged. Dan chuckled.

Shuffling the deck on his propped knee, Toby asked, "Reckon that greaser is still ridin' with the Comanche?"

Dan eyed his pard. "If he ain't scalped 'er, ravished 'er, or shot 'er with my rifle. Reckon by now he's eaten all the provisions too."

Toby studied his cards.

Dan tossed in two pecans. "I feel sorry for Neely Wade. I wouldn't want no daughter of mine runnin' with no Comanche."

"She's a greaser," Toby said, like that explained it all.

With all the pecans on his opponent's side of the playing field, Toby quit. Dan unfolded his body, rose and rubbed the back of his neck. By passing Russ to get to his canteen, he stopped cold and cocked his ear toward the trail.

"Git a move on," he shouted, startling Russ. "Here comes the herd. We need to git with them before the greaser shows up. Be there waiting for her."

Mounted first, Dan was about to make a move when he held up his hand. "Yonder she's comin' now." Drawing his six-shooter, he kneed the paint. "Come on, boys!" he yelled.

At the edge of the thicket, Elena shifted in the saddle, gathered the reins and partially emerged from the trees. Nakiguaht's demand to move back startled her. When she straightened in the saddle Dan's paint flanked by a dun and a pinto came into view. Dan had his weapon drawn and pointed at her.

"This way!" Nakiguaht screeched.

Adrenaline pitched her into a high alert state. Without thought of her actions, she followed him at a full gallop. Neither noticed the cowboy at the head of the herd rise up in the saddle. None were privileged to his grim face, his silent rooting for the trio after the Comanche and the kid, or his worrisome concern gunplay could stampede the herd.

The zigzagging cattle trail gradually took on the shape of an inverted funnel. A funnel made by cattle pointed towards the Red. Nakiguaht glanced back and gave her a Comanche tight-lipped grin of satisfaction. Elena rejoiced in her heart at his signal they'd outdistanced the posse. Choking on grit, she trailed Nakiguaht down to the Red River and the natural crossing used by Indians and buffaloes since time immortal.

At the bend in the river the tail end of Gard's herd crossing was taking place. Behind her she could hear the Jacksboro posse.

The black took to the water after the sorrel. Nakiguaht, veering from a bogged-down steer, checked over his shoulder at Elena. León gave the posse a wide berth and hit the water like a thunder clap. In front of them six mounted Comanches appeared on a bluff to watch the proceedings.

Knee-deep in the current, a log barreled into Ornery. Elena nearly lost her seat as the horse turned sideways. At water's edge, Dan Belcher pointed the gun at her.

"Hold it right there," he yelled over the din of a bogged-down bellowing longhorn. "I got you in my sights."

"Fire that gun and you'll set this herd to runnin'," the trail hand warned in a voice loud enough to be heard on both sides of the Red.

Toby's horse heaved. Russ took one glance at the Comanches and turned green. Dan's mount balked.

Dan hollered, "Bring me my rifle!"

"Dan Belcher," she called out, ignoring his request. "Tell Doctor Farrar Nakiguaht came to his ranch for medicine. He has done nothing wrong. You have escorted him to the Red. That is far enough."

Dan's paint continued to balk. Russ hung over the side of the pinto. Toby's dun gave signs of tying-up. She looked ahead at Nakiguaht on the sorrel climbing out the water. To her side the trail hand had successfully roped the steer.

On the Territory border, the water level was low

enough to climb out without incident. Up ahead, Gard supervised the head count. To her left Nakiguaht, six Comanches behind him, waited and watched.

Elena hesitated. The sucking sound of the steer coming aground caused her to turn back and wait for the trail hand. When he had the steer under control, she rode up by his side.

His glare told her he'd recognized her from the stampede. He would be of no help to her.

Fear and uncertainty took hold. *The Jacksboro posse on the Texas side of the Red will capture me if I cross. Jail for aiding and abetting a hostile Indian off the reservation is my fate. A better fate*, she shivered, *than in the hands of the Comanches. This is Indian Territory and I fear for my life.*

Soon the herd will move on. My plight is of no concern to them. Nakiguaht has never harmed me, but I do not know about his friends. They scare me. I cannot chance it.

The bellowing cattle, horns clacking, had begun to graze forward. The whistling and shouting dimmed. Shoulders slumped Elena stared at the bend in the river.

She urged Ornery through trampled reeds and slick mud to the water's edge. The curve in the wide river slowed the current. A blackjack oak limb aimlessly drifted past. The posse had turned back, but they could not have ridden far, she reasoned, not when their mounts were spent.

The frightful sound of Indian ponies on the move behind her hastened her actions. She called to the dog. Unmercifully, she kneed the jaded black into the water. Too terrified to look back, she kept her eye on the Texas shore.

In a high-stepping choppy stride Ornery splashed the rusty water. Muscles across her shoulders ached with tension. Sunburned hands kept a death-grip on the horse's mane. The threatening crashing of a horse parting waters behind her struck terror in her heart. She kicked Ornery with all her might and leaned over his neck.

Ornery squealed.

A familiar voice resounded. "*Mi amigo*! Come back!"

She jerked up. To her horror the rawhide thong round her neck caught on the saddle horn. The knot of soaked, slippery leather came undone. She clutched her breast, but it was too late. The wooden cross splashed in the water, bobbing and weaving its way downstream.

Ornery swung his head to the side and bared his teeth at Nakiguaht's leg. Elena turned her attention to the sorrel, losing eye contact with the treasure. In a fluid motion Nakiguaht was freed from the saddle and tossing the reins to Elena. Chest deep in the brick-red waters he plunged forward, half-swimming, mostly hopping.

In a daring lunge, he snatched the rawhide thong trailing behind the cross like a water snake. Fisting the cross, he looked back at Elena.

Eyes shining in gratitude, she exclaimed, "Nakiguaht! Thank you. Thank you."

He slid onto the slippery saddle.

Holding out her hand for the cross, she smiled.

Nakiguaht shook his head. "I will hold it for you."

Before she could respond, he'd reined the sorrel away from the Texas side. Elena pointed the black after him.

"Give it back!" she cried.

Concentrating on dry land and a dismount, Nakiguaht refused to answer. Elena followed. From the horse she looked down at him. She did not want to hurt him. His broad face grew sullen. The wet otter pelts round his braids hung limp like drowned furry animals. Elena bit her lip.

"My cross, please." Again, she held out her hand.

Nakiguaht leaned against the sorrel. Meticulously,

he tied a knot in the loose strings. Fingering the cross, he avoided eye contact. At last he spoke. "You cannot go back to Texas. They will put you in a cage."

"I must. I am afraid… my cross."

He held on to it. "There is no need to be afraid. No harm will come to you."

Elena swallowed hard. Her shoulders rose and fell. "What about your friends?"

"They think you are a vision of beauty." He paused, and smiled broadly. "They believe you are mine."

Elena shifted uneasily in the saddle, not sure how to answer. "Did you tell them I belong to my papa?"

For a second, no more, his proud face froze. "I told them nothing," he said, his voice rough.

"Good. May I have my cross now?"

Without a word he tested the rawhide knot. He removed Elena's floppy hat and hooked it on the saddle horn. She leaned toward him. Gently, he slipped the necklace over her head. His dark eyes that missed nothing, gazed at her. "Here is your magic. Does it hold much power?"

The gesture tinted her cheeks. She smiled at Nakiguaht. "It was a gift to me by the padre who taught me. It is my treasure." She didn't add it was the only gift she'd ever received. "Thank you, my dear friend. Now I must go."

"Stay," he said, his voice urgent. "You are safe on this side. We go to the place herds pass. You will meet your father there. Follow me."

Elena stared ahead at the cattle trail scarred by the sharpened hooves of thousands of beeves. Twisting in the saddle, she glanced back at the rusty waters. Up ahead, León trotted behind the sorrel. The hairs on the back of her neck stirred. She said a prayer and headed deeper into the Indian Territory.

By late afternoon the sun pressing down on Elena

had drained the last remaining strength from her body. Ornery's occasional stumble jarred her awake more than once. She could not remember the last time she ate.

Nakiguaht headed due north over high, rolling prairies. Blessedly a patch of blackjack oak appeared on a rise. The smell of the rock-bottomed stream, clear and rippling, put life in Ornery's step. Elena held on as the horse dodged the rough, thick bark of the blackjack oaks and the stout trunks of the cottonwoods.

Stumbling in a stupor, Elena removed the saddle and blanket roll. Her hands fumbled with the hobbles. Under shady cover, she dragged the blanket roll over her knees. Soaked in the river crossing and baked dry by the sun the blanket smelled of dusty mold. Determined to take care of her skirt, blouse and red sash, she unfastened the buckles, unrolled the blanket and spread her meager belongings on the ground.

The tiredness, the soreness of her body overcame the pangs of hunger twisting her stomach. It did not matter. Her leaden legs could not have carried her so much as a yard to food. Her eyelids became heavy. Her head drooped. In a matter of seconds, she blacked out.

***

Ornery screamed. The dog barked. Elena tensed. She could hear discordant mumblings. The moon hidden by the treetops and clouds offered little illumination. Soft padding moccasins headed her way. I will run, she thought. I will run for my life.

A bronze hand touched her arm. Elena jerked around. Face to face with Nakiguaht, she could not speak. Her paralyzed throat emitted strangled gasps.

"Do not be afraid," Nakiguaht said, kneeling beside her. "I sent word to Running Wolf. He has brought food."

She grabbed his hand. "F-f-food? What about Ornery? He is quiet."

"Running Wolf remembered sacks of corn."

101

Elena followed Nakiguaht through the trees. Running Wolf had started a fire. Hand in hand they approached him. Dressed in white man's trousers, a cotton shirt and a dark vest, Running Wolf hunkered by the flames. His long, black braids were wrapped in red flannel. Looking up at them, he grinned.

Innate fears bubbling to the surface, she stepped back into the shadow of Nakiguaht and listened to them speak. Running Wolf's serious tone was hard to deny.

Elena whispered, "What do you talk about?"

"He tells me Fox Eye is the same. White Feather says he does not eat. He grieves for his buffalo horse."

"Who is White Feather?"

"White Feather is the wife of Running Wolf. She sends you a present."

"Me? I do not understand."

Nakiguaht gave a signal. It sent Running Wolf off in the direction of his pony. Elena guarded the frying pan. Twice she had to shoo away the drooling León.

In a nonthreatening manner Running Wolf approached her. Shyly, he handed her a pair of moccasins. The knee high leggings and hard soled moccasins were edged in narrow beading. Silver conchos dotted down the sides.

"They are beautiful," she said softly, tracing the beads with her fingertips. "Tell him I do not know what to say."

Running Wolf's reply set him off in laughter. Elena looked to Nakiguaht.

"He says he made a good trade. His boys chose the best of Nakiguaht's two ponies."

She took a quick breath. "You traded a horse for these boots?"

Nakiguaht's face, partially hidden in the shadows, revealed an awkwardness she hadn't seen before. Warm with emotion, she experienced an urge to touch him and tell him his kindness was overwhelming. Hiding her flushed cheeks, she removed her shoes and slipped the boots on. Trousers tucked inside, she did not wish to cover the beautiful handiwork of White Feather.

Nakiguaht picked up her old shoe, the one he'd slit to accommodate her badly sprained ankle. Turning the shoe over in his hand, he then tossed it aside. Elena caught his eye and smiled.

Heart-filled thoughts bubbled to the surface. *It is said the Comanche do not have hearts. That is not true! Maybe one day I will see Doctor Farrar again. I will tell him Nakiguaht wanted medicine for Fox Eye.* In her mind she began composing a long conversation explaining how she and Nakiguaht stole back Ornery. How he'd saved his dog from a gunshot wound, and how…how…she could not form her thoughts into words for Doctor Farrar. Reaching deep inside, she privately spoke to herself. *Perhaps—no, certainly—Nakiguaht is a true friend. One who has helped me, one I will miss—and one—*She could not go on. *He is Comanche* weighed on her mind.

Harboring the conflict in her heart, she wandered towards a stand of thick trees. On the way back to the campfire she passed her blanket roll. The temptation was too great. She had every intention of resting for only a few minutes.

In the blessedness of sleep she did not hear the mournful *Come a ti yi yippy, yippy yay* wafting across the prairie, or the rustling of the rising Comanches at the campfire.

Chapter Thirteen

an was at wits' end. The very idea of being bamboozled by a no-count greaser made his blood boil.

"That's enough to blister the hide off a Texas alligator." Toby spit out the words.

Dan's lips curled. "Ain't that the truth. A greaser telling me what to do."

Not far from the river, Russ pointed to a grave, a pair of worn boots atop the fresh mound. "Do we have to stay here?"

Toby wandered over to take a look. "It were a Texan, all right. Them boots come from down round Fort Worth."

Dan shut his mind to the boots. He felt uglier than a Mexican sheep. "Boys," Dan began, brain churning. "Where's the closest telegraph office?"

"Red Station has a store and a saloon. Don't know about no telegraph," Toby said.

Moonlight splashed the nearby grave. The worn-out boots took on the shape of a prone pole cat, toe being the pointy head. Russ kept his back to the sight. "There's a telegraph office in Cambridge," he said. "The army put one up two years ago."

Toby couldn't stand it. "Who're you goin' telegraph?"

Dan's eyes nearly disappeared behind the slits. "Fort Sill. We ain't give up yet. I'm goin' say there's a Comanche what's been raiding in Texas. Name of Naki-something or other. He's riding a stolen horse and captured a Meskin woman. We chased 'em onto the reservation."

Russ's eyes popped. "He didn't capture no Meskin. She's with him willing like."

Dan squinted at him. "That don't matter. Ain't nobody goin' believe a red varmin, or a Meskin either."

Toby guffawed.

Russ wasn't finished. "What'll they do to them?"

Dan couldn't believe he was hearing this. He gave Russ a scorching glare. "Who in tarnation cares?"

***

Morning birds chirped. A hornet buzzed over her head. Blinking awake, Elena sensed the presence of a living, breathing body. The moccasins were close enough to touch. Martha Farrar's blanket tossed aside, she sat up.

"You gave me a fright." Intending to say more, she stopped at the misery on Nakiguaht's face. Alarmed, she furrowed her brows. "What is it?"

In a voice taut as a bowstring, he said, "I have seen Neely Wade."

Elena jumped up. Her voice choked. "Where is my papa?"

"He is with the herd. It will pass today."

Confused, she demanded, "How do you know?"

"By the singing we heard in the night."

Elena wrung her hands. "I do not understand. What singing?"

"By the campfire we heard the voice of a white eye. Running Wolf wanted to see the one with the singing song. We did not ride the ponies –"

Elena blurted, "How do you know it was my papa?"

Nakiguaht frowned at the interruption of his story. Biting her lip, she held her tongue.

"We followed the low spirit to the edge of the trail. Two white eyes had captured stray horses from a bad crossing of the waters. One was singing."

He paused; Elena could not breathe.

"The white eye called him Neely Wade."

Joy bubbled in her smile and shined in her eyes. In a merry voice, she asked, "What is my papa like?"

Nakiguaht grunted and looked away. He spoke to the hornet's nest hanging from a cottonwood. "He sits tall in the saddle. His hair is long. He wears a big hat. He rides a horse with white legs." He hesitated, measuring her for a moment. "Neely Wade is a person who wishes to be alone."

Elena lowered her gaze. She refused to accept Nakiguaht's words and before a crackling, popping fire, they ate in silence.

Elena asked, "Where is Running Wolf?"

"He has gone back to where he scars the earth."

"The earth is good for yielding food," she said, handing León a scrap.

Nakiguaht grunted.

Elena downed the last of the coffee, straightened her back and tapped her knee caps. "I will wait here. When the wagons go by the herd will follow and then I will ride out and meet my papa." Eyes shining, she turned to Nakiguaht. "We made it!"

Nakiguaht spoke slowly, his tone flat, "Neely Wade is a troubled man."

Animation left her face. "Why do you say that?"

"He sings the song of a low spirit."

Elena sighed, clasped her slender fingers and stared at them. No longer reddened by lye soap her hands were the color of acorns.

"Please tell White Feather her handiwork is beautiful," she said. When she looked up Nakiguaht had disappeared.

Attention drawn to the horses, she watched him mount the sorrel. Without looking back, he headed for a rise beyond the stream. She could barely distinguish his body beside the horse, or hear the mournful chant floating across the wide prairie.

Seizing a moment of privacy, Elena gathered her clothes and ran to the stream. Nervously, she pulled the skirt over her head before she wiggled out of the trousers. All the while she kept an eye on the whereabouts of Nakiguaht.

At a feverish pace she gave herself a cat bath. Quickly she exchanged the army shirt for her blouse. Nakiguaht's chanting had reached a higher pitch. Her arms goose-fleshed. Barefoot, she sprinted to the base of the tree for the red sash and the Comanche boots. She wound the sash round and round until perfect lengths remained. She looped the knot with care.

Seated under the tree, she picked up the boots and held the soft leather tops to her face. The smell of the rawhide soles reminded her of Uncle Manuel's lariat, the lariat that had switched her legs and never touched Alita's. *Nakiguaht saw to it I had shoes*, she thought, edging her toes inside the tops. *He is kind and...and he helped me. My papa will thank him for that.*

Wagons rumbled and creaked on the trail. A whip cracked. She could hear the driver yell. Elena gathered her skirts and ran to the edge of the trees. Nakiguaht materialized behind her. Turning to him and with her face glowing, she said, "I will pack my horse and come back to the trees and wait. What will you do?"

Nakiguaht mumbled, "Too many sleeps have passed since I have seen Fox Eye. That is where I am going."

"I am sorry you did not get medicine. Doctor Farrar would have given it to you," she said. "He is a good doctor."

His smirk caught her off-guard.

Preparing for departure, Elena hummed joyously. She placed the trousers, shirt, and floppy hat in the middle of the old quilt and the gray blanket. Rolled and buckled, Nakiguaht helped her tie them on the back of the saddle.

Side-by-side, Elena leading Ornery, Nakiguaht the sorrel, they meandered through the trees. Ornery, never at ease with an Indian nearby, pranced and snorted along the way. The dog, head held high, ears perked, brought up the rear.

At the tree-line Elena wrapped the reins around a

low branch and stepped out into the open. Shielding her eyes, she strained for a sight of a slow-moving dust cloud on the trail. Soundlessly, Nakiguaht moved closer to her.

"Listen to me, Elena. Do not go to your father. A troubled spirit lives inside him."

"I have to, Nakiguaht. *I have to.* He is my papa. It is with him I belong."

"Come to Cache Creek with me," he said with grave urgency. "I will not let harm come to you."

"I cannot," she said.

The firmness in her speech left no doubt in Nakiguaht's mind. With a heavy heart, he watched the lone rider on a horse with four white legs. He could hear Elena take a deep breath.

Toe of the Comanche boot hooked in the stirrup, she started to mount, changed her mind and disengaged her foot. Once more she turned to Nakiguaht. The look on his face was so heart-rending she wrapped an arm around his neck.

"God bless," she murmured and kissed his throat. Before he could respond, she was astride Ornery slow trotting across the prairie toward the moment of her life.

The heady sensation of her lips against his throat lingered. He had seen the mates of the blue coats make such a move when the troopers were preparing to leave on patrol. Never had he seen it done in the bands.

She will lift his low spirit. Her courage, her devotion, her warmth will shine like the sun. Her father will love her and take care of her.

His own loss of Elena brought on an overwhelming sadness, a sadness that struck his heart with pain as he watched Elena approach the man astride the horse with four white legs.

Neely Wade had taken to riding alone since the death of Boss. Withdrawing deeper and deeper within himself, he did not relish conversation other than what concerned the movement of the herd. The cowhands didn't joke around him, but, like Boss, they respected his judgment.

Crossing the Red had brought them into Indian Territory, the Territory he hated. He'd been having nightmares again, flashes of the charred cabin, the lifeless eyes of Laurie, her white skull. More than once he'd awakened in a soaking sweat, eyes peeled for bloodthirsty red demons. Last night he'd tried to call out to Laurie in a dream and the words would not come. In the depth of sleep he could not make one sound.

After breakfast he'd ridden out to scout. The hands had the rotation down pat. The wagons had gone ahead. Full of water and grazing, the beeves were moving sluggishly toward Stinking Creek.

The overcast yellow-gray sky reminded him of Tate's prediction. Yep, he declared to himself, we're in for some wind. On a rise he reined up to build a smoke before heading back to catch up with the point rider.

He had his hand in his vest pocket when movement at the edge of the tree-line caught his eye. The devil flew in him as he cursed the Mexican hanging all over a Comanche. He felt like drawing a bead on both of them. At the same time a tree-line could hide Comanches up to no good. He needed to warn the boys.

Horse knee-gripped, he began backing down from the rise hoping to avoid detection, but it was too late. The Mex girl was riding toward him. She appeared unarmed and to his surprise she sang out, "Neely Wade...Neely Wade."

How the tart knew his name cross-fired with the sight of her and the Comanche. There was no doubt in his mind what they'd been up to. His body tightened.

Watching the rider approach, he scrutinized the horse and the yellow cur following, the same handsome black and the dog being chased by what looked like a posse. Hand casually resting on his rifle, he kept an eye on her every move.

Coming up on his side, she repeated as a way of greeting, "Neely Wade."

His green eyes glittered with suspicion. Up close there was something familiar about her. "Yep, I'm Neely Wade all right. How do you know my name?"

"I was told you rode a horse with four white legs, sat tall in the saddle and wore a big hat," she said, a smile spreading on her face.

Her green eyes and the stamp of a Wade jaw brought on a sickening feeling. "That Comanche I seen you with spy on me?"

Elena's mouth flew open. "He is my friend."

"So I noticed." Neely smirked, hiding what he feared was unfolding. "Who are you?"

Flustered, she smoothed the skirt covering her knee. Avoiding his eyes, she said, "My name is"—her voice faltering—"Elena Wade."

The blood drained from his face. In a rough voice, he asked, "Elena who?"

Elena shifted in the saddle. Gathering strength, she said, "My name is Elena Wade, your daughter."

For a time afterwards, he'd wondered if the baby had been his. Now he knew for certain. He stared at the Comanche boots.

"I'd say you was more Lopez than Wade. In fact I'd say you was jest like yore mama. How did you find me?"

"I heard you were with a cattle drive due to cross the Red. I came here to meet you. I thought… I thought… maybe you thought I was dead."

Neely Wade couldn't get his mind off the boots. "All the way from Santa Angela?"

"I came from Jacksboro. Fort Richardson closed. I was a laundress there." She fidgeted with Ornery's mane.

His icy green eyes drilled her. "You came all the

way from Jacksboro by yoreself? That's a mighty long trip."

"Nakiguaht rode part waywith me. He is Comanche, but he is not bad. He is a good friend and he helped me."

Smoldering at the idea a piece of his flesh had hankerings for a Comanche, he bit off each word. "Anybody who has a Comanche for a friend, ain't no friend of mine, let alone no daughter."

His mind centered on dangerous action. If he stayed much longer he would not be responsible. He wheeled the horse around. Kicking dirt grass clumps, he left her on the prairie.

Chapter Fourteen

"Nakiguaht! Nakiguaht!"

Hidden amongst the trees watching Elena with Neely Wade, he spun in the direction of the mounted Comanche splashing across the rock-bottomed stream.

"Nakiguaht! Hurry!"

"Two Bears! What is it?" Nakiguaht shouted, running in the direction of White Feather's brother-in-law.

"Fox Eye takes his last breaths."

Nakiguaht glanced over his shoulder in the direction Elena had taken. Hesitation set in. No longer was his protection needed. Or was it? Quickly, he stashed the canvas sack of corn, removed the blue jay feather and tucked it inside the pouch of jerky. Leaving the provisions partially hidden, he stepped back.

Two Bears called to him again. It was then Nakiguaht leaped upon the sorrel and charged behind the lathered pony. Not far at an old abandoned dugout Two Bears checked up.

After the mounts were hobbled, they entered the crumbling structure for relief from the whistling wind and the blistering bite of grit. Knife drawn, Nakiguaht peered in every shadowy crevice and corner making sure no unwanted varmint shared their space. Satisfied, he looked to his friend.

Two Bears spoke quietly. "White Feather and my wife visited Fox Eye. They could not find him. He had wandered down by the ponies looking for his buffalo stud horse. White Feather told him the stud horse was dead. Three-Finger Kenzie shot him in the Palo Duro Canyon at the last battle. Fox Eye started to shake and mourn for the horse. They guided him to the teepee for rest."

Nakiguaht moaned at the image of Two Bears' words.

"First Running Wolf said you had gone to the Kiowa camp to trade ponies. Others in the band said you were with a Mexican girl. Running Wolf said that was true. He took you food and White Feather's boots."

Nakiguaht waited. When the pause extended, he explained, "I went to Texas to steal ponies for Fox Eye. I wanted to bring him good medicine. That is where our paths crossed. She is gone. Tell me more about Fox Eye."

"White Feather and my wife are with him. He breathes, but he does not come awake. Running Wolf told me where to find you."

"Your pony is spent. I will ride ahead."

Two Bears nodded.

Full dusk was coming on when Nakiguaht rode into the Comanche village. The sight never failed to sadden him. In his childhood there were many teepees. Winding between the remnants and yapping dogs, Running Wolf was leading a pony. White Feather walked beside him. On the back of the trade pony, the boys clung to each other wearing the faces of those in mourning.

The pain of loss seared through him. The sound coming from the depths of his soul was the howl of a wolf caught in a trap. Running Wolf hurried to his side and helped him from the saddle. Together, they stumbled into Two Bears' teepee. Two Bears' wife, Morning Sun, placed a robe around Nakiguaht's quaking shoulders.

Running Wolf said, "We buried Fox Eye under his favorite tree near the creek. We placed his war shield and a pouch of his favorite feathers with him."

White Feather hovered beside Running Wolf. "I watched Fox Eye take his last breath. He did not choke. His spirit had free passage to leave his mouth."

Morning Sun, her voice reassuring, added, "That is true, Nakiguaht. I was there too."

Nakiguaht pulled the robe closer round his shoulders. Wrapped in a private cocoon, he stared at the fire. In one rising and setting of the sun he had lost his love and his father. All the sunshine had gone out of his life. Night covered his heart.

Quietly his friends offered food, drink, and silence. He was glad of that. Talk was not something he could do. His throat was closed. It scared him. If he died with a closed throat his spirit would not have a clear path. It would remain in his body and stay with him in the ground of his burial.

He did not remember falling asleep, but when he came awake he was alone in Two Bears' teepee. Knowing what he must do, he raced toward the sorrel. The saddle and bridle had been left under a stunted mesquite.

Two Bears joined him. "Running Wolf has gone to his place. He says for you to come and see him."

Nakiguaht shook out the horse blanket, still damp from the ride. "That is not where I am going."

Two Bears slipped inside the teepee and reappeared with a dry blanket. He held it out to Nakiguaht. "Take this."

Nakiguaht tried to smile. "We trade."

Morning Sun padded softly to her husband's side.

Nakiguaht tightened the cinch and mounted. His mouth was set in a firm line. "I am going far away to seek a mourning vision for helping powers and a new guardian spirit."

Morning Sun disappeared. When she returned the sorrel had started in a walk. She had to run to catch up. "Here is food," she said.

Graciously Nakiguaht accepted the sack of four hard biscuits, many plums and strips of precious dried beef. He nodded, and with a heavy heart left behind the once proud village.

Nakiguaht tied the sorrel near his favorite bathing place on Cache Creek. The hazy morning fog hung over the waters filtering the sunrays. Focusing on a misty splotch of pale orange shimmering in the middle of the creek,

Nakiguaht began to ponder a location for a mourning vision.

Transported in his mind he was standing on the floor of the Palo Duro Canyon gazing at the lowest cliffs of reddish brown and white layers of mudstone called Mexican Skirts by the white eyes. He tilted his head slightly to take in and remember the formations of orange, purple, brown, and green of the canyon walls. Nestled under a gray and brown sandstone overhang was a spot he considered his until the bluecoats came.

Chief Quanah says a white eye called Goodnight keeps many wo-haws in the canyon. That is not a good place for a mourning vision. If I follow the old trace into Texas to the Medicine Mounds the Rangers will shoot me like they shot my friend who had permission to hunt on his own. He kicked the water.

Wading deeper, he thought of the Wichita Mountains as a site. Daydreaming of an eagle flying over the highest peak, he wondered if the eagle would know he was still a Comanche.

In preparing for the mourning vision as told to him by his grandmother he cleansed himself with care. Going without food would not be a problem for him.

Caught in a web of his own weaving, he relived the moment of goodbye with Elena and the softness of her lips brushing his throat, the shock wave of warmth traveling down his spine. She wanted her father more than him and now like Peta Nocona he would forever remain without a mate. With the deep pain of a broken heart he quietly accepted yet another doom of his dark race.

Destination not firmed, he let the sorrel wander at will to a clearing beyond the creek. Arms folded over the pommel, he lowered his head and prayed to the Great Spirit for a sign.

When he opened his eyes, he caught sight of a pair of hawks, one following the other, swooping over the creek. It was such a common sight he almost turned away. Instead, he found himself drawn to the keen-eyed birds. The one in front banked and sailed over the path of the oncoming hawk in a perfect cross like the one Elena wore. Getting back in line, they carried on. He gave a nod to the disappearing birds and in the twilight world of the half-alive gathered the reins and kneed the sorrel.

***

Elena couldn't stop shaking. Hand outstretched, she cried, "Papa, Papa, please do not go. You... you do not understand."

The blistering wind caught her skirt and lifted it above her knee. Ornery's mane ruffled. Slumped in the saddle and drained of all manner of strength, she did not care if she lived or died. Dreams shattered, and with no place to go, she prayed she would die.

She did not move. Ornery pawed the earth. The dog shut his eyes against the stinging grit. Whistling wind wrapped around her. Still she made no effort to seek shelter. The horse began to walk away. Reins almost touching the earth, he carried her back to the trees and to the stream.

She stumbled through the motions of removing the saddle and bridle and securing the horse. Wind whipped the skirt between her legs; salty tears streamed down her face. León nipped at her heels.

Elena gathered the sack of corn and the pouch of jerky left behind from Nakiguaht's departure. With provisions so precious, she wondered if he was close by. No, she sighed. I do not feel his presence. There is no sign of the sorrel. Ornery is quiet.

Nearby a clump of trees had grown together at the apex. Under the heaven-made covering of entwined branches she huddled against the misshapen trunks, a keen blast mournfully groaning and bending the treetops. At her side León nosed her arm and whimpered.

My papa, my papa, I have come all this way and he did not care. He did not even wish to speak to me. She began rocking to and fro. Her fingers snaked around the cross.

I thought he would be happy to see me. He would explain why he never contacted me. Auntie Rosa said it was a bad storm the night he bought me to her. I always believed he did not think I survived. Neely Wade is my papa. There is no other. His eyes are my eyes. He said I was like my mamma. The whisperings behind the curtain started to come together. Her mother was the one despairing remarks had been made.

Nakiguaht warned me not to go to him. I had to find out for myself. I had to know. She brought her knees up under her chin and wrapped her arm around the moccasin tops. With a free hand, she hung on to the wooden cross. *Gifts, my two gifts*, she sobbed, *the padre who cared enough to teach me and Nakiguaht's gift of moccasins. Why did he not wait for me when he said my papa had a low spirit? He was right. I should have listened to him. Now it is too late.*

Her tears were flowing freely now. *I cannot see myself in the world of Nakiguaht. We have nothing in common. His beliefs are different from mine.* Knowing the admission was dredged from a place beyond logic or reason, she mourned for what could never be.

Shielding her eyes against the morning sun, she peered beyond the sparkling water and through a scattering of trees to the misty prairie beyond. *I have no choice. It is back to Texas to accept my fate. It will not be easy, not without Nakiguaht to lead.* The hawk scrolling the hot updrafts above the stream moved precise and mindless. *A part of things*, she thought, her face drawn. *Not like me.*

At the old campfire site she studied the blackened earth. *A good Comanche*, she mused, *would be able to find tracks and know which way Nakiguaht had gone. Like that mattered. I could never find him. I am on my own. Doctor Farrar was right. The risk was too great. Lives do have a way of changing.*

Beneath the treetops she once again dressed in the army shirt and trousers. Tucking the cuffs inside the Comanche boots, she smoothed the tops with a caress. A fingertip touched each silver concho before lightly tripping over the narrow beading of blue and red.

The burning imprint of Nakiguaht, his quick mood changes, his mystical beliefs and his eyes with the capturing power to both hold her and cause her to back off, would be in her heart for a long, long time. Clamped lips imprisoned a sob.

Approaching horses on the trail quelled the gathering tears from spilling. Ready to spring, she crouched. Ornery gave his warning. An Indian whooped. Another screeched. From behind the trees she ogled four coppery-skinned riders racing each other toward the Red. One pulled away from the others and threw himself over the side of his pony. All but one foot and part of his head disappeared. Elena blinked and the fleeting show of horsemanship was gone leaving behind a dusty stir.

I am trapped! If I go on the trail to the Red I will ride into a hornet's nest. She pondered crossing the stream and coming out on the prairie beyond. *Fort Sill would provide safety, maybe a laundress job. Maybe they will not send me back to Jacksboro and a trial.* On her knees she bent over and wrung her hands. *I do not know where the fort is.*

León nudged her elbow. Wrapping her arm around his thick neck, she whispered, "When the next herd comes by, we will pass them on the side. Let us pray the beeves are stretched all the way to the Red. That is the most protection we can hope for."

First, we eat for strength. Pulling the pucker string, she expected to find jerky, maybe a biscuit. Her breath caught. "Nakiguaht," she gasped, lifting the blue jay feather, bright blue with black markings. Pressing it to her breast, she felt a mystical tie coming from Nakiguaht. *I will not forget you.*

She tripped a finger down the shaft and tenderly smoothed the vanes. A lump lingered in her throat as she removed the floppy hat and stuck the gift in her braid. Digging deeper, she took hold of the nourishment and shared with León.

Hot, glaring afternoon sun came on with a vengeance. Breeze at a minimum, she moved Ornery from the creek to the shade of the trees, ever thankful for the feed left behind.

Towards evening no sign of a herd had appeared. One more night in the Territory brought foreboding. When the tree shadows stretched long across the creek and the night birds quarreled in full chorus, she prepared to wait for dawn and the hope of a cattle drive. *Best to leave the horse saddled*, she thought. *If I have to make a run for it, I will be ready.*

The night wore on and on. The tears for her father had subsided, but, smothered deep down, the silent grieving consumed energy she did not have to spare.

Maybe I should have moved farther away from the campsite. What if I have visitors? León came up beside her panting breaths that smelled of a wild animal meal. Elena cringed; she pushed his slobbering jaws off her arm.

The noises of the night began to fire her imagination. The mere rustling of tree tops sounded like roving Comanches. More than once she found herself holding her breath. Tired, hungry, and strung tight she fisted her hands by her side, her arms as rigid as the flag pole at Fort Richardson. By first light she had yet to experience one second of blessed sleep.

Hail Mary, full of grace, please send a herd with a kind trail boss my way. She made the sign of the cross on her breast, kissed her thumb and looked to the heavens. "Come, León," she called. "We must be ready."

So tired, so very tired, she moved like a zombie. Tossing the rolled blanket across the horse's back was done in a clumsy manner. Mounted backwards, she fumbled with the ties.

Ornery tensed; his signal chilled. Her throat went dry. She didn't have to look. The Redskin rider splashing the water wasn't going to give her much time.

Already in an awkward position, she threw her leg over the horse and slid to the ground. In a crouch she went after the hobbles. The stubborn buckles tested her reserve.

The rider was coming on. Quick as a chased fox she jumped up to mount. Blood rushed to her feet. Fighting a faint, she leaned against the horse.

"Elena, do not be afraid."

Breathing restricted, she stuttered, "Naki... Nakiguaht. You... you came back."

"I came to seek a mourning vision," he said, his voice low and guttural.

"What is a mourning vision? I do not understand." Her voice trailed off.

"Grandmother told me when you lose a loved one you must seek a new guardian spirit. Fox Eye is on his journey to the place behind the sun."

"I wish we could have gotten medicine from Doctor Farrar." Gaining control, she added, "I thought you were there to steal his horses."

To her surprise, he chortled.

"Why do you laugh?"

"I was there to steal his horses. Ponies from the white eyes would have been good medicine for Fox Eye."

For reasons she couldn't identify, she was not taken aback. "And you let me believe you wanted the white man's medicine of a different sort."

"That is true," he admitted. "Ponies from the white

eyes would have lifted his spirits. Fox Eye was dying from the disappearing sickness."

Elena's brows furrowed. "Disappearing sickness?"

Nakiguaht looked to the sky; his shoulders sagged. "The Comanche way is gone. He cannot walk the road of the white man. They remain his enemy. Grief is what took his life."

"I am sorry, Nakiguaht. Change is not easy."

Nakiguaht straightened. "Now you must tell me what happened to Neely Wade?"

She stiffened.

Exercising patience, he waited.

"My papa… my papa did not want me. I must go back to Texas." She pleaded with her eyes. "Will you take me to the Red?"

"He did not want you?"

Elena hung her head.

"He sings with a low spirit. He wants no one but himself."

She kept Neely Wade's revulsion of her being seen with a Comanche to herself. Her mamma was a different matter and not to be discussed.

"Texas is not good. They will put you in a cage. I will take you to the place of Running Wolf. Then we decide what to do."

"Is his place near Fort Sill?"

Nakiguaht frowned. "Is that where you wish to go?"

Elena nodded.

"First we visit Running Wolf. He will have news. I am hunted."

Astride Ornery, Elena wondered why Nakiguaht wasn't mounting up. Having no idea where Running Wolf lived, she wanted to get started. Having a plan energized her.

"What is the matter?"

"It is wise to wait for the sun to greet the sky. The

121

place of Running Wolf is far. We will build a fire and have jerky and plums."

Nakiguaht examined the match in his hand. No longer did the Comanche need a keeper of the flame. He blew on a sputtering spark edging a leaf. Taking his time, he pondered on what lay ahead. *The posse will alert the blue coats over the talking wires. They will track me to the ends of the universe. I have left the boundary and now ride a stolen horse. They will take Elena from me, send her away and trap me in a cage or hang me from a rope. Running Wolf will know what is said at the Fort.*

Elena joined him by the fire. Nakiguaht sucked the pulp from the yellow plum. Laying the skin aside, he said, "Rations are issued every seven suns. On the day called Thursday we travel to the agency. On the next sunrise, beef cattle are turned loose from the corral. Boys and men run them down and kill them with bows and arrows. The following day, we return to our camps."

Elena said, "That is how it is done?"

"It is never enough. We go hungry. After the kill wolves smell blood. They come down from the ravine to scrounge for scraps."

She knew better than to say plant a garden.

Nakiguaht started to check on the horses. He gave a war whoop, turned and grinned.

León growled.

Elena rubbed her arms. "Do not do that."

Nakiguaht feigned a painful expression.

She had to laugh.

Side by side they sat, backs hunched against a tree trunk, to wait for dawn. A wave of apprehension swept through her. *I am scared fate will not be kind to me…and to Nakiguaht.*

That night, and with Nakiguaht close by, maybe too close, his arm touched hers, she slept.

At first light Nakiguaht filled the saddle bag with

plums found along the creek and made sure the canteens were full. Elena pulled out a burr stuck in León's shaggy coat and yanked free a thorny vine wrapped around his leg.

Mind working on the lies to explain Elena's presence in case blue coats crossed their path, Nakiguaht moved in silence as he tied on her quilt.

"How far away is Running Wolf's place?" Elena asked.

"It is a full day's ride."

They crossed streams lined with mesquites, oaks, and hackberry trees. The Wichita Mountains came into view giving the countryside a sense of grandeur. The closer they came to Fort Sill, the more sensitive Nakiguaht became of his surroundings.

He caught Elena pulling down the brim of her floppy hat to her brows for protection against the hot glare. Coming up on a shady thicket, he slowed his mount.

"We rest," he said.

Kicking free of the stirrups, Elena slid from the horse to the ground. Hanging on to the reins, she massaged her temples. Eagerly, she accepted the canteen Nakiguaht offered.

In the direction of a bald knoll León cut a path through short tufts of bunch grass and low-growing prickly pear. In short time León proudly skirted the shady patch, a brown rabbit between his teeth. Nakiguaht gave a high-keyed victory screech.

Elena nearly jumped out of her skin. Ornery squealed.

"Look! The dog caught Mr. Rabbit outside his burrow. See if you can relieve him of our meal."

León growled and shook his head. Fearlessly, Elena reached out for the rabbit. Without making a sound, Nakiguaht came up on the side of the dog. Hands clamped the jaws and pried them open. Elena snatched the prize and handed it to Nakiguaht. As she raked her bloody hand on the dusty ground, the dog, whining, circled round and round her.

"Come. A stream is near. We will have roast rabbit and plums."

***

A fair distance from the weary, hungry travelers a pair of wolves drawn by the offal after the slaughtering of the beeves had prompted bored Calvary officers to declare a hunt.

A large grey lobo sighted by the hounds brought in for the hunt made a mad dash for a steep ravine. Surrounded by the snarling canines, the wolf faced them. Lips outlined in black curled over vicious teeth. A large mastiff with the hunting party went in for the kill.

Fur flew. Blood spewed. After the brutal demise the massive snarling dog clutched the body parts in his jaws. The second wolf, near the first kill, proved to be more elusive. The female had escaped death. Her male companion, father of her cubs, had not been so lucky.

She had to get to her den, protect her litter and signal the others of the oncoming danger. The smell of horses warned they were close. At great speed, swiftly and silently, she entered the thicket. On her toes, muzzle raised, black nose pointed to the sky, she gave a rare burst of barking, followed by a deep-throated howl. Her posture helped carry the call a great distance through the evening air. As swiftly as she'd appeared, she disappeared.

A sharp foreboding shot through Nakiguaht. He grabbed Ornery's bridle. "Stop!" he yelled. "We stop!"

The horse reacted to the unexpected contact. Elena had her hands full. León cut loose with barking. Horrified, she looked to Nakiguaht. "Have we entered a wolf den?"

He reverted to his native tongue. "*Tocusé.*"

His voice scared her. "I do not understand."

"No, I said. The she-wolf was alone."

She started off on Ornery.

Hand on the bridle, Nakiguaht held her back. "We do not cross this line."

Dumbfounded, Elena asked, "Why not?"

"The wolf has warned me of danger."

Brow wrinkled, Elena tried to understand his magic-oriented mind. "Danger? I see no danger."

"The she-wolf tells me bad medicine is ahead."

Nakiguaht backed the sorrel and after he'd cleared the trees turned the horse. Elena faltered. His grandmother had told him his spirit came from the magical mating of the wolves. It was not like she did not know, but to witness his acting upon the omen of the wolf sent a creepy chill up her spine.

"We will go back to the stream near the shady trees," Nakiguaht said.

Elena rode in silence. Hunger, the gamey smell of the rabbit, the long ride and the disappointment of turning back had taken its toll. Twice, she nearly tumbled from the saddle. From time to time, she glanced at Nakiguaht and he seemed lost in another world.

Purple shadows, elongated and distorted, gave a spooky appearance to the previous campsite. Nakiguaht disappeared to round up firewood. Soon a wraith of smoke lazing up from the fire pit and the smell of roasting rabbit brought the dog to her side for his share and a handful of bones.

"You are quiet as a wolf drunk on meat."

Elena pursed her lips. She'd heard enough about wolves to last a lifetime.

"After a kill the wolf will fill his stomach until he becomes dazed. Then he will take a nap. Sleep is his reward. The wolf is my brother. I take heed to his warnings."

Together, they reached for the last plum. Hands touched. Elena drew back like a scalded pup.

"You take it," she said.

"We share."

Elena couldn't resist.

Stars twinkled, birds quarreled, leaves rustled in the treetops. The noise of horses grazing, chains jiggling, was of small comfort to Elena. It was a reminder of the ride tomorrow and what could happen. *If we are separated I will be in trouble. He has looked out for me, showed kindness,* and, despite her thought of him being Comanche, her heart fluttered.

Nakiguaht brought the saddle blankets and the old quilt to the edge of the pit.

She thanked him with a smile.

By the time Nakiguaht realized he was muttering Fort Sill in Comanche, Elena was sound asleep.

As much as he desired her he knew he must wait. Now was not the time. The problems ahead were like the jaws of a puma ready to strike. *Fort Sill will cage me for leaving the reservation. There will be trouble over escaping the escorts,* but the thought of her being sent back to Texas to be trapped in a cage because of him disturbed him most of all.

The morning routine went off without a hitch. Mounts tended to, ablutions taken care of, she waited for a signal from Nakiguaht. On a lark she began braiding her hair. Nakiguaht went to the snorting, pawing Ornery to cut two lengths from the saddle ties and kneeled beside her. He took the ends in his hands and skillfully bound them.

"I watched you braid."

Elena started on the second braid.

Patiently, Nakiguaht waited, leather tie in hand. "It is good to look Comanche. The blue coats will not question you."

Elena swallowed her disappointment. Avoiding blue coats was not on her mind. She'd hoped to please him in another way.

After Nakiguaht had bound the braid, he stuck the

blue jay feather behind her ear, tip pointing downward. To hide her blush she picked up the floppy hat. One glance at Nakiguaht's bare head made up her mind. She rolled the headgear in the quilt and fastened the buckles. Touching the blue feather in her braid, she wished for a looking glass and black eyes.

Chapter Fifteen

gent P.B. Hunt arrived at the Kiowa-Comanche agency on time. At the picket fence in front of the agency, Hunt swung open the gate, crossed the porch and entered his office. The bespectacled clerk hovered beside his desk, pointing out a new circular from the Indian Commissioner.

Hunt digested the message with a groan. The chief duty of the agent, he read, is to encourage Indians to labor in civilized pursuits. The bottom line, he told the clerk, is the agent would be fired if results were not obtained. With disgust he fumed. It is all about money.

Hunt turned to the clerk to comment when a corporal bursting through the door grabbed his attention.

"Telegraphs, sir." The corporal, part of the 10th Cavalry regiment at Sill, announced, "One come through the wires from Cambridge, the other from Fort Concho, Colonel Grierson."

Hunt accepted the yellow-lined sheet torn from a note pad. After a glance, he told the messenger to find Colonel Davidson and tell him he'd see him shortly.

The door banged shut.

The clerk palmed his brow. "Trouble?"

Hunt nodded. "A Jacksboro posse chased a renegade Comanche back onto the Indian Territory. He's on a stolen horse and has captured a Mexican girl."

The clerk shook his head.

***

Elena had been silent for too long. Nakiguaht checked over his shoulder. Weaving in the saddle, she caught his look of concern. "How much farther to Running Wolf's?"

"Not far. His farm is beyond the next rise."

Elena crossed herself. Sun glaring down on her, vision blurred, she regretted not having the protection of the floppy hat. At last a canvas-covered teepee so white against the glaring sun it was almost invisible, shimmered into view.

Elena pointed to wavering vision. "Is that it?"

Nakiguaht grabbed her hand. "Do you want a withered hand?"

His sharp voice, his exasperated expression aggravated her already miserable condition. "I have pointed all my life and my hand is healthy. Explain that!"

"I am Comanche."

His gruff answer prompted her to suggest they rest.

"We are almost there." He kept on.

Hunched beside the rows of dried-up corn sprouts, Running Wolf spotted them. He jumped up and waved. The boys took off in a run to meet them. White Feather rounded the side of the teepee, a large kettle in her hand.

"Nakiguaht!" Running Wolf exclaimed, grinning from ear to ear. "It is good you visit."

White Feather hooked the kettle on the tripod over a low burning fire. "I see who wears my moccasins," she said shyly. Her hand sign, mixed with Comanche, got her meaning across. Arms outstretched, Elena meant to give her a hug. Instead, she collapsed against the comfort of her body. White Feather's soft pats on her shoulder communicated more than words ever could.

"We must eat," Running Wolf said. "Nakiguaht will tell of his adventures since we last met."

Nakiguaht looked to the horses. "Our ponies need feed."

Running Wolf instructed the boys to share the seed corn stored in a lean-to next to the rows of drought-stricken plants. Ornery showed his stuff, but the boys' expertise in handling the horse would've gained admiration from a Mexican vaquero.

What was in the stew offered Elena in a wooden bowl, she did not know. Once she picked animal hair from between her teeth and discreetly set it aside. *Mercy*, she thought. Nonetheless the sustenance began to bring her to life.

Nakiguaht asked about Running Wolf's crops.

Running Wolf bristled. "I wait many moons for a showing. Then the agent said to pull up every other plant. Why plant if you have to pull them up? What is left is dry. No rain falls from the sky."

Nakiguaht frowned.

"Now you must tell where you have been."

The boys inched closer to Nakiguaht, waiting for a story.

Nakiguaht stood, back to the gathering seated in a circle near the tripod. In a surprise move, he faced them in a crouch, head down. When he looked up, the anguish on his face made Elena wince.

He is reliving the death of Fox Eye, she deduced wishing she understood Comanche. He looked to the sky, searching, searching and then he flapped his arms. What followed was a sweeping cross. She watched him trip his fingers up his arm. His expression changed to one of happiness. She heard her name. White Feather laughed. The boys, embarrassed at the love talk, elbowed each other.

Running Wolf disappeared inside the teepee and returned with a pipe and his supply of tobacco hoarded for special occasions. Elena followed White Feather to the stream to help wash the bowls. The boys were wrestling under a stunted mesquite tree, León in the middle of the fray. She heard the oldest one muttering. Coup was the only word she understood. Nakiguaht came up by her side. She took a deep breath.

"Running Wolf and I have worked out the answer if we are questioned. I will say you are the cousin of White Feather and you had been living with an old Kiowa medicine woman. I traded ponies for you. My pass from the agency gave me permission to trade at the Kiowa camp.

The Comanches who saw us cross the red waters will not tell."

Not completely convinced, Elena said, "That is a good explanation, but what if the agency checks the Kiowa camp? The posse could come back." She couldn't bring herself to point out Doctor Farrar may come looking for his horse.

"We will wait for news at the farm of Running Wolf."

***

The patrol picked by Colonel Davidson and without clear direction ambled in a loose pattern. "Sure hope we ain't out here chasing shadows," Corporal Nate James said, spitting a wad of tobacco out the side of his mouth. The brown stream ran down his mount's leg causing the strawberry roan to stomp. Nate checked, saw the damage. "Sorry, old Roanie," he apologized to the animal.

The private next to him groaned. "You need a wife."

The corporal chuckled.

The white officer reined up, pivoted, and joined them.

Nate asked, "What'd ya think, Captain?"

Before he could answer, Brick, the interpreter riding with them, butted in. "Eh, we'll find 'em. Arrest 'im jes like Colonel Davidson said to do."

Captain Andrew Tyler communicated to the Buffalo soldiers with a frown. They wagged their heads in agreement at the disgusting manners of Brick.

Unfazed, Brick kept on. "Yep. Put them leg irons and wrist cuffs on 'im. Throw 'im in the guardhouse. Course, now, that Meskin gal ought go in right with 'im."

Captain Tyler, a stout officer from Virginia, held his temper. "The Mexican is to be sent back to Texas. Orders are to comb the reservation until we find them."

Brick, dressed in buckskins as filthy as their

owner's straggly reddish beard, stood in the saddle and scratched his crotch. "I got a hint where he might be."

The patrol had no choice but to hear him out.

"I seen that Nakiguaht with Running Wolf. They're thicker than ticks on a hound dog. I say we check his teepee for sign."

Tyler gave a deep sigh. "Anybody else got a better idea?" He was met with silence.

The sun making its ascent on the horizon warmed Corporal Nate James as he fussed over Roanie. He made sure the horse was properly groomed and fed before he tended to the captain's mount picketed beside the roan. Brick's Indian pony barred his teeth if he came close. *Did he get his nickname from red hair, or was it because he was dense as a brick?* He figured it was a combination of both.

"Reckon you'll have to take care of your pony yourself."

Brick cleared his throat and let loose with a wad of yellow spittle. Nate frowned.

"Watch your aim," he warned, tempted to pinch his nose at his foul odor.

Brick ignored him. "We're jes a mile or two from Running Wolf's teepee. Care to make a wager we find the renegade and his Meskin girlie on the site?"

Nate, disgusted by the man, hoped he was wrong just for the spite of it. "No, I don't care to make a wager," he said, and started to walk away.

"It was a waste of time riding the territory yestiddy," Brick said, keeping his attention.

In defense of the captain, Nate pointed out it made sense to check out all the possibles on the way.

"We wuz close enough last night to keep on, but, no, the captain wanted to make camp."

If Brick hadn't been assigned to the patrol Nate would have been happier. No sense in getting on the interpreter's wrong side if he could help it, he thought, except every side he had was wrong.

After the last coffee drop disappeared, bacon and hardtack consumed, the corporal, a private, a captain, and one crude soul started out. It wasn't long before the teepee of Running Wolf's appeared on the horizon. No activity was detected.

Brick rode up beside Captain Tyler. "Looks like we're in for a surprise attack. Old Comanche trick."

"There will be no bloodshed," Tyler warned. "Orders are to arrest Nakiguaht and bring in the Mexican girl."

Chapter Sixteen

After Nakiguaht's story telling, Elena wandered about the camp. She tried to picture herself living in such conditions and knew that she could not. Their way of life was so hopeless, more hopeless than a laundress at the fort. It made her sad to think about it.

A niggling in the back of her mind as to where she would sleep began to surface. Inside the teepee were trade blankets atop a deerskin pallet. One, she assumed, belonged to White Feather and Running Wolf, the two smaller ones, the boys. *No matter*, she thought, *I'll sleep outside on Martha's gray and black cover.*

She was headed toward the horse and her blanket when, tail curled tight over his back, León barked. The boys searched the skyline. Running Wolf came out of the teepee, looked at the dust stir in the distance. Nakiguaht joined Running Wolf.

Running Wolf squinted. "Blue coats, I count three, one more in buckskin."

Nakiguaht ran for Elena. "Get inside," he ordered in a sharp voice. "Do not come out. We must know what the bluecoats want. White Feather stays with you."

The closer they came, the more fiercely León barked. Both boys hunched beside the dog and stared at the riders. Bluecoats never brought good news.

"Think they cut rations because the corn died?" the youngest asked.

His brother shrugged.

Nakiguaht stood next to Running Wolf, watched and waited. He recognized the buckskin rider as the louse who hung out at Evans Store. They had the look of a patrol on a mission. He felt their eyes on him.

The closer the patrol of two colored troopers and a white officer came, the more Nakiguaht reverted back to old ways. Tempted to go for Running Wolf's bow and arrows, he had to control himself. He had Elena to think about. The accompanying of the buckskin rider spelled trouble. Dreading what could be unfolding, he turned to Running Wolf. His stoic expression revealed nothing. León came up beside Nakiguaht and faced the riders, growling and snarling.

Nakiguaht watched the interpreter point him out.

Weapon drawn, Captain Andrew Tyler shouted, "Nakiguaht, you are under arrest. Raise your hands over your head."

From within the teepee White Feather had her hands full holding on to Elena. Strength came from within. She broke free.

Brick snickered. "There she is." He looked to Nate James. "What'd I tell ya."

"Tell him to raise his hands," Tyler instructed Brick.

"Put yer bloodthirsty hands over yer lice infested head," Brick muttered in perfect Comanche. He signed for emphasis.

"What are the charges?" Nakiguaht demanded.

The captain looked to Brick.

"Says he ain't done nothing."

"Tell him he's being arrested for horse stealing and capturing a Mexican girl."

"He did not!" Elena screamed.

Captain Tyler leaned forward in the saddle. "I see you speak English. Don't worry. We will make sure you are safe."

"I am safe! I am the cousin of White Feather. Nakiguaht traded ponies to the Kiowa medicine woman for me."

Brick couldn't keep still. "She lies like all Meskins."

Captain Tyler twisted in the saddle, and caught sight of two good-looking horses hobbled near the withered corn patch. "We'll take them to Agent Hunt. It's his job to sort it out."

Weapon still drawn, the captain ordered Nate and the private to tie Nakiguaht's hands behind him. Uncertain about the Mex girl, he hesitated. It was enough. Brick stirred dust covering the short distance and took a rough hold of Elena.

Nakiguaht went berserk. The scuffle did not settle until Nakiguaht had landed a solid kick to Brick's groin, Elena had scraped the side of his face with her fingernails, and León had a mouth full of buckskin fringe.

Brick swiped at the blood trickle on his cheek. "Damn greaser," he swore. "Leastways she ain't got no knife. If you ask me she's in on the horse stealing too. Lookee that black. It ain't no Comanche or Kiowa pony. It come from Texas."

Ornery and the sorrel were brought to the fro, saddled, and with the prisoner and the Mex girl mounted, the patrol headed for the Indian Agency.

The unmerciful sun glared down upon the Comanche family beside the teepee. Running Wolf shielded his eyes and stared at the shimmering backsides of the horses and riders fading in the distance.

"My friend is in bad trouble."

"What will happen to them?" White Feather asked, a catch in her throat. "Nakiguaht is in much love with Elena."

Running Wolf glanced at his pitiful corn patch and then at the canvas covered teepee. He slumped like all the air had been sucked out of him.

"Will Nakiguaht come back?" the oldest boy asked.

"I do not know," his father answered.

Tears in his eyes, the youngest ran behind the stunted mesquite tree.

***

The farm of Running Wolf soon disappeared in the

blistering glare. Nakiguaht side-glanced Elena, her hand clutching the cross. He knew his story had flaws, *but Elena is safe. She has a bill of sale in her belongings.*

"All's I wuz goin' do wuz see if'n she had a knife," Brick kept on. "Never knowed a Meskin what didn't pack one."

Nate, the private and Captain Tyler rode in silence.

"They'll stab ya in the back every time."

The captain glared at him. "That's enough, Brick."

Hands bound behind him, and being led by Nate on the roan, Nakiguaht slouched in the saddle. *In the white eyes' cage I will rot. Never again will I cast my sight upon Elena.* Sorrow welled up from his depths. He threw back his head, stared at the blistering sun and howled like a wolf over the death of a mate.

Horses balked. Captain Tyler reined up, hipped around in the saddle and stared at Nakiguaht. Nate had his hands full with the roan. The private's horse reared. Elena started for Nakiguaht. In a twinkling of an eye, coupled with a remarkable feat of horsemanship, she wedged her horse next to his. Ornery showed the whites of his eyes.

"They think you stole horses and captured me." Her Spanish came out in a screech.

Before he could answer, the corporal riding behind shouted, "Git away from him."

Elena refused.

Captain Tyler brought the party to a halt. Allowing no nonsense, he rearranged the horses, Elena on one side, Nate leading Nakiguaht on the other. He kept the private in the middle. Brick insisted on riding stirrup to stirrup with Tyler.

Hot and dusty, scorching wind blowing in her face, Elena hollered up ahead to the captain, "Where are you taking us?"

The wind swept away some of her words, but the captain got the gist. "To the Indian Agency," he yelled over his shoulder.

To the beat of Ornery's gait, Elena picked up the mantra, Kiowa medicine woman, Kiowa medicine woman, Kiowa medicine woman. She couldn't get it out of her head. *What if the agent knows better? Brick is nasty. He cannot be trusted to translate truthfully. He will do what he can to make Nakiguaht look bad.*

Elena tried to catch Nakiguaht's attention, but the thick neck of the private's horse, the dark blue of his arm and torso, the bobbing yellow scarf at his neck blocked her vision.

On and on the patrol and their captives traveled. Pounding hooves, squeaking leather, snorting horses whistled through the windy, hot air. At a stream the captain halted for the grimy party to wash the grit from their throats and allow the horses to drink. Cans of peaches were opened and passed around along with hardtack. The private offered to start a fire for coffee. At first the captain refused. Groans followed and he relented.

Try as she may, she couldn't get close to Nakiguaht. If it wasn't the private blocking her way, it was the corporal keeping Nakiguaht, the roan, and the sorrel, away from the group. Elena avoided Brick. León growled at his foul-smelling enemy.

By the time Captain Tyler ambled over her way, the patrol was preparing to mount up. Despite his dusty tall boots, grit-covered azure pants and dark blue shirt he carried himself with all the dash of a cavalry officer.

"It's not much farther," he said, offering her a leg up.

Unassisted, stirrup toed, Elena swung on the back of Ornery. From the horse, she looked down at him. "Nakiguaht did not capture me," she said, her voice cracking.

The stout Virginian officer drawled, "The agent will straighten it out."

The kindness in his eyes gave her a nudge of hope.

Dusk was coming on. Elena tried to stay focused. By the time they reached the white picket fence of the Indian Agency every bone in her body ached. Tension pulled at her muscles.

Captain Tyler brought the patrol to the edge of the fence and instructed Nate, Brick, Nakiguaht and Elena to come inside with him. He ordered the private to stand guard with the horses and to keep his eyes open in case trouble erupted with the prisoner.

The clerk hunched over his desk. Agent Hunt had paused in his letter writing to the Indian Office complaining about the lack of rations. He held his head in his hands. Both looked up at the sound of horses at the fence and boots stomping on the porch.

Captain Tyler entered first. He held the door for Elena, Nate, hand on Nakiguaht's shoulder, and Brick. Once inside, all faced Hunt.

Hunt rose, rounded the desk and leaned against it. Arms folded, he gave a deep sigh. As much as he was relieved to have the Comanche in custody, he knew his day, already a long one, wasn't over.

"Where'd you find him?" he asked.

Tyler shifted the rifle strap at his shoulder. "Running Wolf's farm."

"Did he offer any resistance?"

"None we couldn't handle."

Brick spoke up. "He attacked me, the louse-infested devil. Him and his little girlie here."

Elena bristled. She fired back, "He touched me."

The close quarters of the agency left much to be desired as far as breathing was concerned. Brick stank up the place. Elena started to move as far away from him as she could get.

"Hold it right there, Missy," Hunt warned. He turned his attention back to Tyler. "Did you find any horses?"

"A sorrel. The Mex girl is riding a handsome black."

"It ain't no horse I've seen in any of the camps," Brick butted in.

Elena's heart plummeted.

"Where did Nakiguaht capture you?"

Elena tried to read Hunt's expression, find something encouraging in his voice. "He did not capture me."

Hunt's attention shifted to Brick. "Ask Nakiguaht where he got the sorrel."

Elena watched spittle drool from the side of his mouth as he placed his tongue over the top of his teeth to produce guttural Comanche.

"Where'd you steal the sorrel?" Brick growled.

"I trade," Nakiguaht said quietly.

Brick looked to Hunt. "Says he don't remember."

This is not what we planned. Her Spanish came into play. "Did you say you did not remember?"

Nakiguaht eyes narrowed. "I said I trade."

"Brick lies," Elena shrieked her voice full of fury. "Nakiguaht said he traded."

Brick gave a hideous laugh. "The girlie lies. She said he traded ponies to the Kiowa medicine woman for her."

Hunt frowned. "Let us start from the beginning. Tell us your name and how you came to be in the Kiowa camp."

Elena fought the bile rising in her throat. "I am Elena Wade, the cousin of White Feather. I live with the Kiowa medicine woman. Nakiguaht came to trade ponies. We were on our way to Sill when Nakiguaht was arrested. He stole no horse. It was part of the trade."

Before Hunt could reply, she turned to Nakiguaht. Hands bound behind him, he stood tall and straight. She started telling him what she had said when Hunt interrupted.

"What hold does this Comanche have over you? Has he threatened you?"

Elena grabbed the cross. "It is the truth."

"Are you afraid?"

She stared at Hunt.

He changed tactics. "Tell me about the black horse."

Captain Tyler joined in. "She calls him Ornery."

"Is that his name?" Hunt asked.

"*Si,* that is his name. He does not like the smell of Indians." Too late, she bit her tongue.

"Then it is not an Indian pony. Where did it come from?"

In a panic, Elena turned to Nakiguaht. "What must I say about Ornery?"

"No more Spanish, Elena Wade," Hunt instructed.

She took a deep breath and exhaled slowly. "I do not know where the horse came from. It was part of the trade. The Kiowas did not like him."

Hunt did not believe her. If anything he looked more disgusted than ever.

"Nakiguaht, I have been told, is known for his story telling. Did he tell you to say this? Your explanation does not add up. One more time, does this Comanche have a hold on you in some way? You are safe here."

"What I say is the truth."

Hunt rounded his desk, and rummaged through some papers until he found a yellow-lined sheet torn from a notepad.

"What you say is not the truth. We received a wire from"—he glanced over the paper—"Cambridge. A Jacksboro posse, the captain being a Dan Belcher, alerted the agency they chased you and Nakiguaht from Texas to the Red River. Nakiguaht was on a stolen horse and had captured a Mexican girl."

Elena blanched. She started shaking.

Nakiguaht lunged for her.

Nate pulled him back.

Captain Tyler drew his Colt.

The door burst open. Colonel Davidson's adjutant rushed in. "Sorry to interrupt"—he glanced around—"but the Colonel sent me for you. Colonel Grierson's here from Fort Concho. There's an impromptu wedding party at Davidson's. Grierson's playing the fiddle, big goings on. Your presence is requested."

"Thank you," Hunt said, relief in his voice. "I'll be there shortly."

As soon as the adjutant left, Hunt turned to the group facing him. Tyler had Nakiguaht at a standstill.

Brick was beside himself. "I told ya they ain't nothing but a bunch of liars, both of 'em."

Hunt ignored him. "This will have to continue in the morning. Take the Comanche to the guard house. Have him put in leg irons and cuffs."

Tyler nodded. "What about the Mex girl?"

Hunt scratched his chin. "Lock her in the back warehouse. Put a guard at the door. Make sure she gets something to eat."

The captain, weapon holstered, said to Nate, "Keep a bead on him. I'll take care of the Mex girl."

Nate shoved the Comanche in front of him, boring the Colt nose in his back. "Tell him to get a move on, Brick. He's going to the guard house."

Brick snickered. "Yer're going to jail, yer red devil. They're goin' throw away the key."

Despite his tied hands, Nakiguaht managed to flash Brick an obscene gesture from behind his back. Brick went for him. He was easy prey for a punch in the gut. Not expecting cast iron resistance, Brick drew back a sore fist.

The captain gave a stern warning, enough so that Brick backed off grumbling. Nakiguaht called him a coward. Nate shoved the barrel tip deeper into his back.

The door banged shut. Elena stumbled to a nearby chair. Arms folded across her knees, she pressed her forehead against them. Her shoulders quaked. The cross dangled in her lap. The clerk came forward and offered her his handkerchief. Elena shoved him away. There were no tears left in her body.

The captain came to her side. "Come on," he said, his voice gentle.

Elena raised her head. "Nakiguaht did not capture me."

"He is gone, now. You have no reason to fear him."

"I do not fear him. Don't you understand? He is my friend."

He took her by the arm, helped her from the chair, steered her through the door and to the outside entrance to the warehouse. In passing the private standing guard he instructed him to take care of the mounts.

León looked to the horses and back again at Elena.

"Please," she said. "Let the dog be with me."

The musty room smelled of stale air and a dead rat. Empty hardtack boxes stacked in one corner, a cot, bare ticking showing, shoved against a wall, and a three legged chair completed the furnishings.

What appeared to be a rickety framed window was deceiving. Stuck fast, it wouldn't budge. León, nose to the slanted, grimy floor, sniffed until he a dragged the partially decomposed rodent from under a box. With no air stirring, he sat on his haunches and panted.

Elena kicked the offensive object across the room. Back at the window, this time with a chair leg, she banged around the frame. Chinks of plaster fell to the floor. Worked loose, she shoved the cloudy paned window upwards and propped it with the chair leg. A gust of oven-hot air blew in her face. She could hear the movements of the guard and knew he was watching the window.

It wasn't long before a key scraped in the lock. A private handed her a basket of fried bacon, army bread, a canteen of water, and a necessary bucket to put under the cot.

Dark now, she had to feel her way around. Benumbed, she sat on the edge of the cot. León, interested in the basket, wagged his tail. She could make out his bright eyes and hear his panting.

Shadowy movement passed the window.

"Yer got that Meskin in thar?"

Elena froze at the sound of Brick's voice.

"Yep. I'm guarding her," the private said.

"Why don't you turn yer back? I can git in the window."

"Can't do that, Brick. It's against orders. Nobody's allowed in."

Brick snorted. "She's a regular wild cat. I want me some of that."

León picked up a deep throated growl.

"She got that dog in thar?"

"Don't matter if she's got the dog, or not. You ain't going in."

Elena's heart thudded in her ears. She couldn't breathe. It seemed an eternity before she heard the shuffling off of Brick and the audible groan of the private.

Ears perked, head cocked, the dog pawed her knee.

"Oh, León," she croaked. "We are in such trouble."

He pawed again.

Elena dragged the basket in her lap. "You are hungry."

After handing the dog a thick strip of bacon, she automatically brought the bread to her lips. Head tucked, she made out the outline of her moccasins in the shadowy darkness. Heart heavy as a round stone, she touched the blue jay feather behind her ear and fingered the leather ties.

"It is all over," she told the dog. "I have lied to the

agent and he knows it. Tomorrow our fate will be decided."

Thoughts of the outcome brought to mind the sickness of Fox Eye. *All has disappeared from me too, my papa, Auntie Rosa, Uncle Manuel and Alita. In the morning they will take Nakiguaht. I will be sent back to fade away in jail for aiding and abetting a renegade.* She did not want to cry, but she could not hold back the scalding tears cascading down her cheeks.

León whimpered.

Chapter Seventeen

W ith all the fanfare of tossing a carcass in a meat wagon, Nakiguaht was thrown in the basement solitary confinement cell. Leg irons dragged the floor. Cuffs kept him off balance. Unable to brace himself, he landed in a heap against the wall. The guard tossed a blanket and a bucket inside. The heavy door of three layers of wood reinforced with iron strapping grated shut. The guard peered through the small, barred window.

Nakiguaht rose slowly and leaned against the wall. It was not the first time an Indian had been locked up. He saw the circular pattern on the stone floor made by the dragging leg irons of a pacing brother caged like an animal. On the wall a white man had scratched counting marks. The small barred window above slashed the remaining rays of twilight.

At daybreak his fate would be settled at the Indian Agency. Prison or hanging, he wasn't sure. Without Elena, it did not matter. The sun had gone out of his life.

He took a deep breath to steady himself and thought of a time not so long ago. When the warriors came in and surrendered they were caged in the old ice house. Once a day, raw meat was thrown over the high walls. Some prisoners were kept in a cell under the barracks. Fox Eye survived to die of sadness.

He would die, too.

Anger took over.

Nakiguaht began checking the restraints.

Holding up his arms he let the cuffs dangle. He tried pulling his arms apart. I will be like Satank, the old Kiowa chief. He had courage. It is a better to die with honor.

Not for the first time, he wondered how, in a wagon full of bluecoats on the way to the Jacksboro jail, Satank had managed to sneak in a knife and cut his wrists in such a way the cuffs fell off. Freed of restraints, the Kiowa chief grabbed a carbine and made a final stand. It cost him his life.

Nakiguaht put his teeth to the fleshy part of his wrist. He drew his hands together as tightly as he could. Lips, dried and cracked by the blistering wind of the ride, poised over his flesh. *My teeth will be my knife. Yes, I will be like Satank.*

At the council tomorrow I will tell the agent I captured Elena. They cannot accuse her of helping a Comanche. She did not steal the black horse, I will say. There are papers in her belongings to prove it. She will be set free.

Sorrow welled up within him. If he did not release the anguish churning inside, he would die before he had a chance to free Elena. Head tilted back, he howled. The death chant followed. The volume of his voice filled the cell, rose to the ceiling and rained down on him.

The racket caused a face to appear in the door window. "Shut up, you heathen," the guard ordered.

Nakiguaht got his meaning, hung his head. Quiet as death, he remained so until the break of day.

It was anything but quiet at Colonel Davidson's private quarters. Colonel Benjamin Henry Grierson, Commander of the Tenth Calvary, fiddling away, tapping his toe, had his audience clapping hands, singing along and the wedding couple dancing.

Tall, swarthy Ben Grierson tugged at the full beard hiding a facial disfiguration. Having been kicked in the face by a pony as a child had left him with a scar and a mighty distrust of all equines.

If it weren't for the horses coming to Sill from Kansas he wouldn't have made the journey from Fort Concho, but he was determined to have first pick of the mounts for the Buffalo soldiers under his command. Resentment of allowing coloreds to join the Regular Army brought on the constant battle of looking out for his troops.

147

Supplies for them were the shoddiest and the mounts, nags.

The wedding party brought to mind his own wedding to Alice Kirk, his wife of twenty-four years. If it had not been for their strong attraction, she'd never have married a man who was not a devout Christian. Over the years she'd tried to convert him. Always he admired her religious scruples and always he wanted her, like tonight.

Ladies in their swishy dresses, hair done up with the help of curling irons, fussed around the table. They kept the punchbowl filled, pies and ginger cookies on the side. They talked about being behind in fashions, the conditions of their living quarters and about dear Helen, a favorite among the wives, having lost her father.

Even with the windows wide open, the air was close and soon Ben Grierson put down the fiddle and refilled his punch cup. Hunt joined him. Together, they discussed the never-ending Indian problem.

"For instance," Hunt was saying, "this evening another renegade was arrested. He'd been in Texas and besides stealing a horse he'd captured a Mexican girl."

Grierson downed the punch cup contents before he replied. "Any depredations?"

"None I'm aware of. A Jacksboro posse sent a wire alerting us the pair had entered the Territory. What's disturbing is the Mex girl is lying through her teeth. I don't understand. She acts to me like the Comanche has some kind of hold over her."

"Send the Comanche to prison in Fort Leavenworth," Grierson suggested. "The herders that brought in the horses will be leaving tomorrow. Escorts and the prison wagon can go along with them. Safety in numbers as they say."

"Our prison wagon is in disrepair. What about an improvised freight wagon?"

Grierson shrugged. "Fine with me."

"The girl is going back to Texas. Jacksboro can deal

with her," Hunt said, concluding the conversation.

Chapter Eighteen

T he next morning León wanted out. Elena called from the window to the guard.

The key grated in the lock. The barrel of a carbine poked through the cracked door.

"The dog can come out," the guard said, "but I ain't letting him back in."

Elena nodded. León shot between the blue-clad legs and took off for the nearest tree.

The door squeaked shut and the lock clicked in place. Like a signal being sent, the sound brought with it the hard cold fact. They were caught red-handed, and she knew it.

She wanted to wash, look her best for the sentencing, but that was not to be. The most she could do was straighten her clothes, tug on her braids and wait. The six o'clock reveille had already sounded for roll calls and the mounting of the guards.

Soon the door opened for a private to take back the basket and hand her a tin plate. This time, she had cold beef hash, old bread, a plum, and a canteen of coffee. She sat on the edge of the cot with the plate in her lap.

Her sigh lapsed into a moan and, from a moan, dovetailed into a familiar chant. A chant she'd heard Nakiguaht sing. It rose from her depths and escaped from surprised lips. It was as if she'd breathed on him. Tears trickled down her face.

In full uniform the new officer of the day marched with the old officer to the guardhouse. Together, they checked the roster, taking turns peeking in the window.

Nakiguaht could hear them discussing him. From the tone of their voices and his smattering of English he had a good idea what they were saying. The door grated open, a tin plate of cold beef hash and a hard biscuit was handed him. A bucket of water and a dipper was unceremoniously deposited at his feet. The guard appeared nervous to be in the same cell with him. Nakiguaht raised his arms, made a face, and rattled the cuffs. Shaking in his boots, the officer of the day backed out the door.

Nakiguaht squatted beside the vitals and ate, tasting nothing. He picked out a floating spider before he filled the dipper. Wishing for war paint, and as if he were free, outside in the sunshine, a touch of warmth passed over him. He did not move a muscle, or blink an eye. A magical butterfly touch from Elena had brushed his heart. It was gone as quickly as it came. Nakiguaht remained still, hoping for more, but in his heart he knew it was over.

He was in just such a position when the escorts came for him. The leg irons were removed and the handcuffs were changed from the front to the back. The two accompanying guards prodded him along with rifle butts.

"If he runs, I'll shoot," the stubby nosed private, forage cap askew, said.

"He ain't gonna run," the second guard announced and jabbed him in the back.

From the window Elena watched a corporal join her door guard. They chatted, pointing to Agent Hunt making his way toward the white picket fence. A nervous little clerk, a sheaf of papers clutched to his breast, hustled to keep up.

Behind the pair, Captain Tyler had Brick by the arm, dragging him along, his gait definitely alcohol influenced. Approaching from the opposite direction, Nakiguaht, scowl on his face, and two guards stepped along briskly. Ushered outside, she started for Nakiguaht's side. A hefty hand clamped her shoulder and pulled her back.

In charge, Captain Tyler posted one of Nakiguaht's guards at the gate, and instructed Elena, Nakiguaht, and the stubby nosed private to go inside. Brick stumbled across the porch, braced himself at the door frame and tripped inside. The captain went in behind him. Hunt leaned against the front of his desk.

Hunt made eye contact with Elena. "Okay. Now, start from the beginning and tell the truth."

"Nakiguaht, what must I say?"

His sullen eyes gazed at her. "I stole a horse. I captured you in Texas."

"Enough Spanish," Hunt ordered.

She covered her face with her hands. "No, no, no," she muffled, wagging her head.

"What hold does this Comanche have on you?" Hunt demanded.

Elena refused to remove her hands.

Hunt turned his attention toward Brick. "Ask him what he was doing in Texas. Why was the posse after him?"

Brick belched. He called Nakiguaht a *taen taet.*

Hunt snarled at Brick. "No foul name calling. Do you want to be replaced?"

Brick straightened up and translated Hunt's question.

Nakiguaht replied, "I was captured in Texas. I escaped escorts taking me back to the reservation. I stole the horse."

Word for word, Brick repeated Nakiguaht's answer.

Elena gasped. *He is hanging himself.*

"Ask him where he captured the Mex girl."

The Comanche talk went back and forth.

Sober-eyed now, Brick looked to Hunt. "He says he captured her on the Chisholm Trail. He wuz goin' to bring her back and show her to his daddy, but his daddy is dead."

It is all over. Why is he doing this? She felt a cold fist closing over her heart.

"One final question. Where did the black horse come from? Did he steal it too?"

Elena stole a glance at Nakiguaht, pleading with her

eyes for a sign of why he was saying these things. *Did he not know he was hanging himself?*

Brick did as he was told. Nakiguaht took a long time in answering. Elena held her breath. *What is he saying?*

Brick scratched under his armpit, coughed, shuffled to the door and opened it. He crossed the porch and spit over the rail. Back in the office, he swiped his hand across his mouth. "This here Comanche says the black belongs to the Mex girl. He says she's got papers to prove it. Thar're in the quilt tied on to her saddle. But that ain't all. He says to free her. She ain't done nothin' wrong."

Elena sank to the floor, hugged her knees, and buried her face. Hunt went to her and placed his hand on her shoulder. She jerked away from his touch.

"He can't hurt you now," he said in a consoling manner. "We will see to it you're taken back to Texas safely."

Green, glittering, wet eyes flashed at him. "I don't want to go to Texas. I want to stay here. I can be a laundress… I can cook…"

"There is no place for you at Fort Sill, Elena," Hunt said gently. "I am sorry."

"But… but what about Nakiguaht?" Confusion spilled in her voice.

"He is going to prison at Fort Leavenworth. Horse herders from the fort are returning in the morning. Along with escorts from Sill, they will travel together."

Her eyes grew as big as the parade ground sundial. "For how long?"

"For more than a few years. You will have to stay guarded until it is convenient for us to escort you to Jacksboro."

***

Mounted on a red chestnut gelding, Doctor Farrar glanced back at the pony trailing behind on a rope. The

153

tales told in the saloon by the returning posse, Dan Belcher in particular, were disturbing. Martha said it didn't matter what condition Elena was in, he had to bring her back with him.

The dun picked up its gait. *Son of a gun*, Farrar thought, *that pony knows he's close to home.* The yellowish brown parched grass crunched, the sun boiled down on him, his arthritic knee ached, all of which made him grateful the Indian Agency wasn't much farther. He'd been told it was easy to find. Look for a white picket fence and a trading store nearby.

Farrar mumbled good morning to the guard wiping his brow, dismounted, and glanced around before opening the gate and crossing the porch. He knocked and entered.

Agent Hunt glanced up from his desk. "Can I help you?"

Curious, the clerk put down his pen and shoved his spectacles up his nose.

Farrar extended his hand. "I'm William Farrar, doctor out of Jacksboro. I came here to see if I can find out something about an Elena Wade. She's a Mexican American supposedly captured by a Comanche."

Hunt accepted his hand. "You missed the inquiry."

"What do you mean?"

"Have a seat, Doctor Farrar."

William Farrar pulled up a chair close to Hunt's desk, brought his leg across his knee and plopped his sweaty Stetson on top. Hunt started with the wire from a Dan Belcher, Jacksboro posse.

"What got me was how easily the Comanche confessed to horse thieving and capturing the girl. He's leaving for Fort Leavenworth prison tomorrow morning."

"What kind of shape is the girl in?"

"Looks fine to me. She started off lying through her teeth. It seemed to me the Comanche had some kind of hold on her. A threat"—he shrugged,—"something like that."

Farrar filled in Hunt with his connection to Elena and Nakiguaht, dwelling at length on the way Nakiguaht had saved his foal. He ended with a request to see her.

***

No air stirring, Elena pulled the gray flannel shirt from the waist band and fanned herself with the tail end. Twice she'd hollered out the window to the guard about her dog. Both times he'd said he had not seen hide nor hair of him.

She couldn't settle down. Settling down meant thinking and she didn't want to do that. Her whole being was like it didn't exist. She was in somebody else's body living a bad dream.

The knob jiggled, the door scraped. Slumped on the cot, Elena refused to look up. William Farrar closed the short space separating them. "Elena," he said, "I have come to take you home with me."

Elena jumped up, fists clenched by her side. "Doctor Farrar," she cried. "Nakiguaht did not tell the truth."

Hunt filled the door frame and listened. The guard remained outside, hovering behind Hunt. Farrar took her hand in his.

"Tell me what happened," he said kindly. "Did you find Neely Wade?"

"It is like you said. Too many things had happened in his life. He did not want me. Nakiguaht said he was a low spirit."

Farrar huffed. "That's a shame."

"Nakiguaht said he captured me, but that is not so."

"Suppose you tell me what happened."

Elena had a trace of hope in her voice. "Nakiguaht came to your place for medicine for Fox Eye."

"Fox Eye is his father," Hunt put in. He scratched his chin. "How did he know where to find the doctor?"

The agent is making the same mistake I did, she

thought. *I will not say what kind of medicine.* "It is known Doctor Farrar had removed a bullet from a Kiowa. Doctor Farrar saw to it he had a fair chance to return to the Indian Territory, but he escaped from the escorts. He wanted medicine. Our paths crossed on the Decatur road."

Farrar waited. At last, he encouraged, "Go on."

"Nakiguaht was worried harm would come to me on the trail. He followed me."

"Did he harm you?"

Elena shook her head. "No, Doctor Farrar, he protected me and... and..."

"And what?" Farrar wanted to know.

Elena blushed. "Now we are... uh, good friends."

Farrar chuckled. "I'll be damned."

"Why did he say he'd captured you?" Hunt asked.

"Because I would have been jailed for aiding and abetting a Comanche off the reservation. He wanted to clear me of charges."

Farrar smiled at Hunt. "I'll vouch for Elena. Sounds like a misunderstanding to me. Why don't you set him free and let him get on with his life?"

"Sorry," Hunt said with quiet emphasis. "I can't do that. Nakiguaht left the reservation. That is a very serious offense. When he had a chance to come back, he escaped. I can't reward him for such behavior. It would encourage others in the band to do the same, or worse. Don't forget, he's on a stolen horse too."

Farrar frowned. "That's not completely true. He borrowed my sorrel to ride back to the territory. I have his dun pony. It was a trade."

"Nakiguaht and his guards will come by the office in the morning for paper work to take to Leavenworth. The best I can do is to let you and Nakiguaht have a few minutes together at that time."

Hunt started to leave, but turned back. "I've got one more question. Where did the business with the Kiowa medicine woman come from?"

Elena could barely speak. "Nakiguaht made up that story to explain my presence on the reservation."

"Oh, I see. Well, then, until the morning."

After Hunt left, Farrar lingered. Elena told him about Ornery being stolen and the gunshot wound to the dog. When he admired her boots, she told him with a catch in her throat Nakiguaht had seen to it she had shoes.

***

Nakiguaht, leg irons back on, paced the pattern left on the stone floor by a previous occupant, an Indian brother no doubt. The cage suffocated him, made him choke, the air was not free. The military prison at Fort Leavenworth would kill him, if this cage did not first. Of that, he was certain. He'd seen wagons pulling out from Sill with prisoners in leg irons and cuffs. An escape attempt would mean death.

Sweat poured from his body. Ankle blisters burned, his wrists rubbed raw. He couldn't sit still, he had to keep moving.

He kept at the pace, working himself into a frenzy. All through the night the dragging of the iron chains sounded like demons on the warpath following him, taunting him.

At sunrise, he was found by the guards slumped in the corner. It took constant prodding, tugging and pulling, accompanied by a steady stream of cursing, to get the scowling Comanche to his feet.

The door guard released Elena. P.B. Hunt waited at the gate. William Farrar, having spent the night with Captain Tyler, had arrived on his chestnut leading the dun. All eyes were on the approaching wagon drawn by four mules.

"We could use some rain," Hunt said, watching the dust cloud created by the mules.

"That's a fact," Farrar agreed.

Elena hung back.

Tearing round the side of the building, León made a bee-line for Elena, barking, tail curled over his back. When the dog spied Farrar, he licked his boots, his hand and the side of his pants.

"He's a big hit down at the stables," the door guard said. "Sleeps with a tall black horse."

Jingling traces, the crack of a whip, snapped Elena's attention back to the wagon. Clearly she could see three soldiers on a bench facing Nakiguaht. One soldier was by Nakiguaht's side. He looked to be a sergeant.

Hunt disappeared inside the agency.

Farrar stepped back and put his arm around Elena.

The brake screeched. The mules began to blow. Nakiguaht had his back to her. In a flash she broke free from Farrar and grabbed hold of the wagon side, splinters digging in her hands as she hoisted herself over the top.

"Nakiguaht," she garbled, checked herself, and garnered grit. "Nakiguaht," she repeated stronger. "Doctor Farrar is here. I am going back to Jacksboro with him."

Nakiguaht remained silent.

"You can find me there," she said, wishing he would speak.

Farrar stepped to the side of the wagon. "Tell him the foal is doing fine. I named him Comanche."

Elena put on a smile and relayed the message. She watched his expression remain unchanged. He did not utter a word.

"Ask what does he want me to do with his dun?"

She saw his eyes widen ever so slightly at the mention of his pony.

"Give my pony to Running Wolf."

Hunt bustled next to her. Over the top of the wagon board, he handed a brown envelope to the sergeant. "The Comanche's papers," he said, glanced at Nakiguaht, and stepped back. Elena was helped out of the rear of the wagon.

The driver, lines gathered, released the brake. Whip clutched, he cracked it over the mules' backs. The wagon creaked and rumbled away.

Elena wrung her hands and stared after it.

Nakiguaht could not look back. That she would be cared for removed the last obstacle in his plan.

A shadow of a hawk passed over the floorboards sending shivers up his arms. He knew what he had to do. In just such a wagon on its way to a Jacksboro jail, loaded with bluecoats, the Kiowa chief had caused his own death. Like Satank, he would do the same. Never could he live in a cage.

Chapter Nineteen

Colonel Benjamin Grierson arrived at the stone corral bright and early. Cavalrymen in white cotton duck overalls and unlined protection coats had already picketed the horses on a sturdy rope in front of the stables.

The brisk morning air inspired the equines to squeal and nip at each other. The men, anxious to be ready for inspection, made quick work with curry combs and brushes. Colonel Grierson kept his distance. He'd wait until 'stand to heel' was completed.

Watching his mount on the line, he worried about the animal. It was the one beast he was comfortable with. So far every knowledgeable horseman at the garrison had checked the horse and found no reason for the change in behavior, or its way of going. Maybe this morning he'd have some luck. In all his years in the cavalry, he'd never had a mount he'd liked except this one.

To pass the time, Grierson observed a lieutenant helping a novice recruit with the art of grooming.

"Lieutenant," he called, keeping his distance from the picket line. "Do you have time for a question?"

On his way to join Grierson he yanked hay from the neck opening of his stable frock. "What can I do for you, Colonel?"

Grierson pointed to his bay. "He's a bit lame and I was wondering if you'd take a look."

"He's been checked by those who know more than me. Tell you what, there's a doctor from Jacksboro here. He's got some problem with the Indian Agency. He's there now. You might want to ask him before he leaves."

Grierson agreed and waited for the lieutenant to choose a mount, throw on a saddle and hand him the reins. Ben Grierson climbed aboard, hoping his skittishness didn't show.

160

***

Hunt, Farrar, Elena, and the door guard watched the wagon until it became a speck of dust. "I'm sorry, Elena," the doctor said. "Martha and I will be pleased to have you with us."

Elena noticed the crinkly lines around his eyes, the kindness shining in them. She tried to smile, say something, but no words came.

"I didn't have a choice," Hunt said. "You'll be better off in Jacksboro."

Chin tucked, Elena blinked at the toes of her moccasins planted in a bed of parched grass. She didn't dare open her mouth. Like the Comanche, she would not show the white man her feelings.

Hunt had his hand on the gate, the door guard waited nearby, and Farrar was asking Elena if she knew the whereabouts of Running Wolf when the approaching mount riveted their attention. Elena noticed the unusually tight grip the officer had on the reins of the well-broke cavalry horse.

Hunt gave a grin of recognition. "Morning, Ben. Welcome to the Agency."

Grierson dismounted awkwardly, nodding to the guard to hold the horse. "I'm looking for a Jacksboro doctor."

"That's me," Farrar said. "What's the problem?"

"Actually, it's my horse. He's gone lame on me. No one seems to be able to pinpoint the cause. I was wondering if you'd take a look. I'm real fond of the fella."

"I've doctored a few horses in my time, but I doubt I know any more than the others. There's one person who might be capable of solving such a problem."

Excited, Grierson exclaimed, "Who is it? Where can I contact him?"

"It's a Comanche by the name of Nakiguaht. I know of his amazing talent first hand."

Elena's heart skipped. She brought her hands to her mouth.

"Where can I find this Comanche?" Grierson asked.

"Problem is he just left on his way to Fort Leavenworth prison."

"Hmmmm." Grierson tugged at his dark full beard, the beard covering the childhood scar.

"If it was me," Farrar continued in his most persuasive voice, "I'd send this guard up ahead with orders for the wagon to turn around and head for the corral. It wouldn't hurt to have the Comanche take a look. I'm telling you, he's remarkable."

Elena caught the gleam in Farrar's eyes, the hope in Grierson's. Hunt hustled inside the agency and returned with a notepad and pencil. Using Farrar's back to support the pad, the colonel hen-scratched *Return Prisoner to Corral* and signed it Colonel Benjamin Grierson.

The stone corral had loop holes at intervals. Some said the holes were for ventilation, others, to give the mules a view. Too many times crafty Indians had boldly stolen stock. Elena thought the corral had the look of a fort.

While they waited for the return of the wagon, Grierson led the bay around for Farrar to observe. Hunt and Elena watched the proceedings. Farrar pointed out the horse was favoring his right hip.

Before further observation could take place, the rumble of the wagon took their attention. Elena stood on her toes, trying to see Nakiguaht as the mules made their entrance.

The sergeant ordered the halt beside the group. A gangly soul with a thick brown mustache surveyed the area with one silver gray eye. He kept the other on his prisoner. Grierson approached the wagon and instructed the sergeant to remove the shackles.

Elena watched the proceedings. Knowing Nakiguaht was not aware of what was happening she ran to the wagon side.

"Nakiguaht."

He jerked around, causing the sergeant to drop the key.

"You were brought back to examine Colonel Grierson's horse. Doctor Farrar told him you were good with horses."

"I do not..." The sergeant yanked the chains, throwing him into a stumble.

Doctor Farrar came to Elena's side. "Tell him his talents are needed."

Elena smiled, and did as she was told.

Those concerned with the horse, plus a barrel-chested private with a swollen jaw holding a water bucket, gathered round. The language problem dictated Elena would assist Nakiguaht with the horse. None were aware of Farrar's meager grasp of Spanish, or Nakiguaht's scant understanding of English.

"I thought I'd never see you again," he said.

"Oh, Nakiguaht, what are we to do?" Hands touched and lingered over the lead line.

Throat-clearing and coughing went on behind them. Colonel Grierson had to smile. At a distance he couldn't hear the conversation yet he recognized the tender expressions on the faces of the Comanche and the Mex girl.

Nakiguaht tried to concentrate on the horse's gimpy gait as Elena walked the horse away from him, but for the life of him, he couldn't keep his eyes off Elena. It stirred him in such a way he knew he could not live without her. Knowing he'd never see her again, he'd stretch his time with the horse.

Nakiguaht glanced at the audience gathered behind him. Except for the sergeant, the bluecoats from the wagon, Hunt, the Colonel and Farrar all wore the look of expectation. To the side, the bucket holder's curiosity kept him anchored.

Nakiguaht asked for a hammer. Elena passed on the request. The bucket holder disappeared briefly. When he returned, he handed a ball peen to Elena. Cautiously, he backed off from the Comanche.

With all the patience bred in him, Nakiguaht lifted each hoof, and tapped around the sole. Next, he examined the legs for swelling, pain, or any abnormality. Elena at his side, he treasured each precious moment. Savoring her nearness, he moved in such a way his arm brushed hers, a thumb raked her knuckles, a hand cupped her elbow. The tenderness warmed her face and touched her heart. Silently grieving with hopelessness, she returned the subtle contact.

"We're going to be here all day," the sergeant griped.

Pulling rank, Grierson shot him down. "This is my last ditch effort for this horse. If it takes a week, so be it."

Nakiguaht flexed the fetlock joints in the front end, examined the hind hocks, always keeping an eye on the hip.

"I will pray to see you again," Elena whispered.

Nakiguaht grimaced. "I will not be coming back."

Elena bit her lip.

His request for the water bucket raised the eyebrows of those watching. By standing on the upturned bucket, he was able to look down upon the horse. Starting behind the ears, he began massaging with the heel of his hand, inching his way down the horse's neck.

"Ask Doctor Farrar to watch the mouth. When he licks his lips, let us know," Nakiguaht said as he moved the bucket beneath the withers.

Farrar stepped forward.

Nakiguaht caught the puzzlement on his face. "Tell him my grandmother said when a horse licks his lips his pain has disappeared behind the sun."

The doctor made eye contact with Nakiguaht and nodded.

Mid-way of the back, the Comanche closed his

eyes. Softly chanting, he checked each vertebra of the back bone. The closer he came to the hip area, the louder he chanted. Cracking one lid enough to gauge the white eyes' uneasiness, he almost laughed at himself. They were in for a surprise.

Nakiguaht moved the bucket close to the right hip. He told Elena to lift the right hind leg and pull back when he gave the signal. He positioned his hand over the hip.

"Now," he instructed.

Simultaneously with the pull, he thrust the palm of his hand on the offending hip area. The action produced a loud cracking sound of a freed joint.

Farrar exclaimed, "He licked his lips!"

Elena walked the horse for all to see the marked improvement in his gait. A round of applause broke out. Even the sergeant joined in.

Colonel Grierson clapped again. "I'm taking this Comanche back to Concho with me. He's too valuable to rot away in the Leavenworth prison manufacturing cavalry boots and shoes."

Hunt hesitated. "He's prison bound."

"I know. The Indians are your responsibility. Can't you think of a loophole?"

Hunt grinned. "As a matter of fact, I can. A bit of a stretch, though."

"Let's hear it," Grierson said.

"I received a circular from the Indian Commissioner encouraging Indians to labor in civilized pursuits. Even went so far as to suggest employing Indians over whites where feasible. They want rations to decrease."

Grierson laughed. "For economy's sake, far be it from us to prevent a decrease in rations. I say that's good enough. He's going back with me as an aide for the horses, mine in particular. I'll requisition pay for him."

He turned to the impatient sergeant with the bushy brown mustache. "Tell the Leavenworth horse herders the prisoner won't be joining them."

The upbeat tone of voices, the joy on Elena's face and the departure of the wagon befuddled Nakiguaht. He looked to Elena for an explanation.

"You have been hired by Colonel Grierson to take care of his horse. He will pay you."

"I am not going to prison?"

"No, you have been saved by Colonel Grierson."

Taken first by suspicion and then wonderment, he couldn't respond other than to look upon Elena in awe. Elena gently plucked the blue feather from her braid. She took his hand in hers, placed the plume inside and closed his fingers over it.

"Think of me," she said, her voice quivering.

Numbed by her action, Nakiguaht remained at a standstill, so touched by the feel of her hand in his he couldn't utter a sound.

The trusty sorrel back in Farrar's hands and the dun returned to Nakiguaht finalized the last detail as the entourage left the corral. Elena watched, heart in her throat, until the last speck of dust settled.

In a storage room stashed between buckets and pitchforks, Elena found her tack, quilt and Martha's old blanket. Ornery was easy to spot in the turn-out area. León was right behind him.

Doctor Farrar suggested they freshen up at Captain Tyler's quarters before starting back to Jacksboro. He'd spent the night there and the captain's wife, Mary Ann, was as hospitable as her southern husband. Elena silently rode beside him.

In an effort to engage her, Farrar said, "I don't know how Dan Belcher got the idea you were captured. It will be my pleasure to straighten him out when we get back to Jacksboro."

"I have been charged with aiding and abetting a renegade. That is what awaits me."

"Don't worry. I will take care of it," Farrar said in his authoritative tone.

Elena thanked him and returned to her own world.

Chapter Twenty

Colonel Grierson had made short work preparing to leave Fort Sill for Fort Concho. He'd commandeered four horse herders from the Fort Leavenworth entourage and given them charge of the new top of the pick mounts for the men in his command.

His sense of humor and his ability to get along with the Buffalo soldiers made Grierson a favorite among his men. Before mounting up, he had the troopers introduce themselves. Nakiguaht remained suspicious.

Using the excuse his horse needed rest the colonel climbed aboard the ambulance and made room for Nakiguaht. It was hard to communicate with the sullen Comanche and from time to time he side-glanced the hunched figure beside him. On one such glance he glimpsed the feather Nakiguaht held in his hand, the feather he'd seen tucked in the Mex girl's braid.

Smiling to himself, he recalled the love he had for his wife. In some ways their beliefs were worlds apart, but that didn't harness the feelings they had for each other.

He tapped the driver's shoulder. "Turn around. We forgot something." To the trooper riding beside the ambulance he issued orders for the horse herders to hold up and wait for their return.

Nakiguaht displayed all the signs of bolting. Grierson checked the panic in his eyes and realized what must be going through his mind.

First, he pointed to the feather and then in the direction of Fort Sill. Next, he cupped his hand and brought it to his chest. Scrutinizing Nakiguaht's face to see if he understood, Grierson noticed the gratitude in the Comanche's eyes. It was something to behold.

The rattle of the ambulance brought Farrar, a ginger cookie in his hand, Mary Ann and Elena to the window. Elena burst through the door, Farrar right behind her. Mary

Ann gathered her skirts and followed.

Disembarking from the wagon, Grierson looked to Farrar. "We forgot somebody."

"What do you mean?"

"I need the Mexican girl. If she will, I'd like to take her back with me. My wife could use some help with our quarters and somebody needs to teach this Comanche."

Elena's heart thumped. She wore such an expression of happiness Farrar's throat caught. Stetson tipped forward, he scratched the back of his neck. "You're getting a mighty fine pair."

In the flurry of activity, Farrar checking Ornery's hooves, Grierson and the driver helping themselves to a basket of ginger cookies Mary Ann had brought out, Nakiguaht steered Elena behind the wagon.

He offered her his outstretched palm, a feather cradled within. "*Mi amigo, it is you I cannot forget.*"

She had to take a deep breath. Taking the plume from his hand, she tucked the feather in her braid.

Her eyes sparkled. "It is good you are taking a step on the white man's road. Colonel Grierson says I must teach you."

A faint light twinkled in the depths of his. "And what is it you will teach this Comanche?"

As if he could read her mind, she shyly turned aside.

Activity broke the moment. The driver gathered the lines. Mary Ann and Farrar waved as they boarded the ambulance wagon. Glowing, Elena returned the gesture. At her side, shoulders thrust back, Nakiguaht stood tall.

Thanks to the colonel León had the taste of a ginger cookie on his tongue, and with his nose pointed toward the ambulance wagon and the colonel's stash of cookies inside he trotted behind the black horse and a dun pony tied to the back.

About the Author:

Gaby Pratt is a member of Romance Writers of America, an associate member of Western Writers of America, Women Writing in the West and both Texas and Montana Historical Societies. She has taught in the Virginia public school system and in Delaware at a Christian Academy. She and her husband live on the farm in the First State, where they raised their children, horses, a few cows, and too many barn cats.

Social Media Links:

Website: http://www.gabypratt.com/

Goodreads: http://www.goodreads.com/author/show//2700287.Gaby_Pratt

Facebook: https://www.facebook.com/gaby.pratt.9

Pinterest: https://www.pinterest.com/gabypratt9

LinkedIn: https://www.linkedin.com/pub/gaby-pratt/6b/795/56b